RICHARD ALLEN
SUEDEHEAD

Richard Allen was the pen-name of James Moffat, born in Canada in 1922.

Moffat was prolific, though one repeated claim that he was the author of 'at least 290 novels in several genres under at least 45 pseudonyms' still requires independent verification. It is known that Moffat contributed to an early draft of the novel *Somewhere in The Night*, which was later completed (or entirely rewritten – sources differ) by Michael Moorcock and published under the pseudonym Bill Barclay in 1966.

However it was Moffat's gritty youthsploitation novels, all written in the 1970's under the name Richard Allen, that form the bulk of his legacy today. The Joe Hawkins story began in *Skinhead* (1970) and was continued in *Suedehead* (1971). Later there were further instalments in Joe Hawkins' story, as well as novels focussing on other youth movements such as *Smoothies* (1973), *Punk Rock* (1977) and the final Allen novel *Mod Rule* (1980). Altogether there were eighteen novels under the Richard Allen brand.

James Moffat spent most of his final decade in obscurity, though he lived to see the reissue of the Richard Allen novels in the early 1990's. He died in July of 1993, while living in a nursing home in Newton Abbot.

Also by Richard Allen

Skinhead

RICHARD ALLEN

SUEDEHEAD

With an introduction
by Andrew Stevens

DEAN STREET PRESS

INTRODUCTION

Beginning with *Skinhead* in 1970 and culminating with 1980's *Mod Rule*, the Richard Allen novels, published by the New English Library, bookended what was in many respects a dark decade and inadvertently comprised one of the most comprehensive documents concerning the post-mod evolution of the skinhead subculture. However, even for the most ardent of fans, it is the first two titles in the cycle, *Skinhead* (1970) and *Suedehead* (1971), which act as the best introduction to the New English Library (NEL), a cornerstone of literary pulp.

Richard Allen was the pen name which Canadian writer James Moffatt toiled under for *Suedehead* (1971), a sequel written in response to *Skinhead*'s entirely unexpected success and which would help perpetuate a market for the likes of *Skinhead Escapes*, *Trouble for Skinhead* and *Skinhead Farewell*, though, as even die-hard fans will attest, the plots began to wear thin.

In *Suedehead*, Joe Hawkins' milieu shifts from Plaistow in East London, with its "poverty and hardship", to a West End pad and dalliances with more affluent women, where he's all of a sudden stepping out wearing a bowler hat. But what we're dealing with is a more enigmatic prospect than *Skinhead*, as suedehead itself represented a more tailored approach to the skinhead aesthetic, with its velvet-collared Crombie, houndstooth check suits and brogues. The hair grown out and lack of bovver-boot attire singlehandedly and conveniently for many to this day manage to sidestep any visual associations with the far right – though for Allen, the look still represented "cultism" as a façade for violence, which was of a "deep, dark nature".

Four decades on, it is perhaps the debut solo single of Morrissey which serves as a blistering arpeggio-laden intro to the subculture for many, certainly representing an enduring fascination with aspects of the East London demi-monde on the part of the post-Smiths singer. The musical taste of skinheads and suedeheads themselves ran to reggae and ska, reflecting their broader interest in West Indian culture and fashion. Trojan Records returned the recognition with their 2008 *Suedehead* box set. It's arguably a footnote in the evolution of the skinhead subculture but Barney Platts-Mills' lauded *Bronco Bullfrog* (1969) represented the suedehead style's sole depiction in cinema (though it's often mislabelled a "mod" film).

Interest in the NEL, Allen and the *Skinhead* cycle remains strong and testimony to the enduring values and aesthetic of the skinhead subculture, demonstrating perhaps that dangerous youth cults incubating within the bourgeois system prove a perennially potent concept. No doubt fuelled in part by successive iterations of skinhead, the cycle of novels was repackaged two decades on in the early 1990s by *Skinhead Times* as a six-volume set (which included other Allen titles such as *Knuckle Girls* and *Punk Rock*). Beyond the odd enthusiastic write up in *Scootering Magazine*, Moffat, who died in 1993, would probably be surprised to know that the spirit of his work lives on, not only in the form of films like *This is England*, but also allusions in the work of contemporary bands such as Sleaford Mods. Not a bad legacy for a middle-aged writer for hire living by the Devonshire seaside.

Andrew Stevens, May 2015

SUEDEHEAD

CHAPTER ONE

As HE STOOD in the dock, Joe Hawkins considered his situation with utter detachment. Legal procedures meant nothing to him. He had done a police sergeant and now he faced the consequences of that action. What *they* – those stupid bastards going through the motions of justice – did not know was how all this was making him an even greater figure in the eyes of his pals.

Joe listened to snatches of the case against him. He was not troubled about the outcome. It was always the same – a fine, a warning, publicity. He returned the magistrate's glare, he smiled cockily at the coppers in court. He refused to assume an innocent attitude. Nobody was going to say that Joe

Hawkins ever knuckled down to authority. He was a law unto himself.

Suddenly, Joe felt tension mounting inside him. The message reached his shocked brain. This wasn't any common or garden fine. Not the way that old buzzard was talking. This wasn't a warning to behave like other decent citizens. This was the big walk – bird...

"...*eighteen months*..."

Joe was stunned.

"*You may step down. Next case...*"

Stumbling from the box, Joe felt strong hands grab his arms. Realisation smashed into him like red-hot daggers probing for a vital spot. Eighteen days was a lifetime but months sounded like the total end of all his dreams. The gang would forget him in a few weeks. When he came out there would be nothing for him to command. Some rotten bastard would have taken control and he – the famous Joe Hawkins – would be a skinhead without mates.

"He can't..." Joe struggled. "He bloody can't do this!"

"That's where you're wrong," a harsh-voiced policeman said. "You've got off light. If I had my way..."

"Nobody arsked for your opinion," Joe snarled, striving desperately to keep his cool.

The policeman grinned and motioned for the others to remove this *object* from the courtroom.

He had no sympathies for those who deliberately attacked coppers. The magistrate had surprised them all with his treatment of Joe and, the bobby thought, *about time too.* Practically every member of the force believed that stiffer sentences would eliminate eighty percent of the injuries they sustained doing their duty.

Joe's co-ordination vanished as his legs turned into elastic. He felt weak, ready to scream. Half-dragged, half-staggering, he made it downstairs into the cells. According to one of the fuzz he had a short wait – and then..."Clobbered you, eh?" a thin-faced youth smirked as he picked at a sore on his ear. "I got three years."

Joe shuddered. "I expected a fine."

"That's the way it goes, mate. It all depends on how the beak's missus treated him the night before!"

"What did you do?" Joe asked unemotionally.

"Knifed my girl," came the easy reply. "The little bitch held out on me." Blood trickled down the ear and a dirty handkerchief was hurriedly used to stem the flow. "We had an agreement how much she would charge, then I discovered she was upping the ante and keeping the change." Narrowed eyes surveyed Joe's face. "You ever tried pimping?"

Joe's head shook a fast negative.

"Man, it's the life. They do all the work and you collect."

Something about the youth frightened Joe. Not a physical fear but a deeper menace which went against his grain. Not many things bothered Joe but pimps were scum and their treatment of girls they professed to care for left him cold.

"I once had a black chick..." The youth kept talking, evidently proud of his record. He was about Joe's age yet there was a worldly wisdom in those narrowed eyes which went with his thin, hungry, cunning face. Every so often he examined his blood soaked handkerchief and nodded.

Joe lost interest after the first few sentences. He had problems of his own and how this other prisoner had spent his freedom did not matter. Nothing mattered except those eighteen months inside. Could he take it? Could he emerge feeling like Joe Hawkins of old? Or would prison have a sapping effect on him? He knew several old lags near his home and hated to think he would ever look like them.

"...and you can have her address if you like."

Joe shook his mind awake. The youth had not noticed his preoccupation.

"Man, she's a terrific worker. Six, seven marks a night. That's money, man."

"I'll give it some thought," Joe said.

"Do that, mate. You'll be out long before me. I'm not going to get remission."

"Why not?"

The youth laughed. "I've done porridge before. I'm not worried about it. I like breaking every rule in their book."

The hell with that! I'm going to get full remission, Joe thought.

"Stick with me," the youth said softly, eyes wider and shimmering now. "I'll show you the ropes..."

*

Standing on the street with the Scrubs a gigantic horror behind him, Joe Hawkins took a gulp of air down into his starved lungs. It wasn't that this air tasted fresher, or had less pollution in it than the air breathed back there in Wormwood. It was just that here, on the outside looking in, there was a freedom quality he had been denied for far too long.

"You goin' my way Joe?" Nobby Clarke asked as he hefted his bundle under one ancient arm.

"Naw," Joe replied thankfully. He did not want to be seen anywhere near the old lag. It had been great finding somebody he knew by sight in prison but once outside he was determined to avoid all ex-cons like a plague.

"Lemme give you a tip, Joe," Nobby said brightly. "Never get nicked for anything small. Next time make sure they gets you for a big job!" The old man shuffled a few feet, turned and grinned. "Go see that woman I mentioned. She'll help a kid like you!" He winked and hurried off.

Alone now, Joe thought back to the first day of his bird. That had been bad but not nearly anything like when he discovered he was a special target of every queer in the Scrubs. God how he loathed those bastards! He had always figured homosexuals to be small, dancing men with carefully manicured hands, lisps and a walk that signposted their aversion to women. He had found that they did not belong to any such tight limitation. Some of the ones who had tried to lure him into their cells were big, strong, typical heavy types. One especially had been sent up for murder – a vicious ex-boxer with a protection racket backing his penchant for desirable young men.

The queers had been bad but they had not been the worst of his problems. Even now, after all that porridge, he could not get used to regimentation and loss of identity. The soul destroying routine had shattered his self-confidence until Mr. Thompson had seen fit to take Joe under his wing. In a sense, Joe felt a debt of gratitude to Thompson. As a screw he was a pretty good egg. But he was a screw! And although he had gained permission for Joe to take a course in office procedure, and got him a job in the prison administration section, there was that barrier – prisoner and screw!

Some of the old lags had been kind, tolerant of youthful mistakes, eager to pass along knowledge gained from years spent doing prison sentences. Nobby had been most helpful. Thanks to him Joe had managed to evade the dirtiest jobs and make sure his lapses weren't reported.

"Never again," Joe whispered to himself.

Far ahead, Nobby shuffled along – a lonely, beaten old man with but one thought gnawing on his saturated mind; back to Plaistow and the boozer. Joe didn't give Nobby more than a few weeks freedom. The man was beyond rehabilitation. He'd blow his bankroll, make a couple of visits to Social Security and then, when the boom was lowered, he'd do a sloppy job and get nicked again.

Now take me, Joe thought. *I'm young. I'm smart. I'm not going to commit a crime like Nobby. I've got an address and I can make out okay until I get a job. There'll be birds and booze, but not another visit to the Scrubs.*

Taking his time, Joe walked in Nobby's wake. He knew exactly where he was going. The magazine article had shown him the root. Skinheads were dead, man. Phased out. Home had never appealed. All his life he had dreamed about a plush flat somewhere in the West End. So now he would make the leap from poverty street into the affluent society. In one gigantic jump. The advice poured into his ears by all those old lags had taken root. If he was to succeed he had to plead, and beg, and make like a downtrodden slum-dweller whose environment had been the root cause of his imprisonment.

They must be stupid, he laughed silently as he began to whistle.

CHAPTER TWO

BERNICE HALE had known poverty as a child and this made her extremely susceptible to the pleas of those whose homes she could associate with her own background. When Joe Hawkins entered her pathetically small office she felt an immediate "relationship".

"Mrs. Hale?"

"Sit down, Joe. Relax. I'm here to help you – not scare the hell out of you!" She smiled and waved to a chair.

Joe sensed the desire to get on friendly terms. It was just as Nobby had said it would be. He sank into the chair and returned the woman's smile. After serving his porridge he needed to look at an attractive woman and think about some of the girls he had known before that old bastard of a magistrate handed him time.

"You've been a model prisoner," she said with blue eyes scanning the dossier.

He nodded, judging her to be around fifty. She was slender enough to be a movie queen and her vital statistics left nothing to be desired.

"I've a son your age," she said, fixing him with an expression that vaporised all his notions of an easy bit. "Being in prison sometimes makes a *man...*" and she stressed the man, "yearn for female company. I'd advise against hasty decisions, Joe. You're not in any position to spread kings yet."

"Nobby Clarke sent me to see you..."

"I have a dozen Nobby Clarkes on my books, Joe." She got to her feet and breathed in deeply. Her breasts thrust against a woollen jacket. Her eyes caught his, and air whooshed from her lungs. "That was silly wasn't it?"

He continued to stare.

"Joe – get those ideas out of your mind." She came around her desk, hitched her skirt and sat half on, half off the edge of the desk. Her stockinged legs enticed, provoked, sounded clarion calls in his frustrated mind. "I'm being a tease, I know. But then..."and she laughed huskily, "I always am."

He could not make head nor tail of her tactics. She seemed to be begging for him to make a move. Yet, was she? He did not dare risk it. He sat hard on his chair, perspiration beginning to roll down from his armpits.

"You pass!" she said briskly and extended a slender hand. "If you had made one move to assault me that would have been the end!" She shook his hand, and hurried back behind the desk. "I've a thing about sex maniacs. I don't like them!"

"I only came here to ask for help, Mrs. Hale."

"I take it that means money?"

Joe nodded. He was confused by her tactics.

"For a room?"

"Yes. I don't want to live at home."

"Why not?"

He shrugged. "Reasons..."

"Name a few!"

"I've been inside. I don't want to go back. My parents would crucify me."

"I see..." She consulted her file. "You were a vicious monster, Joe. Skinheads are, unfortunately, a product of our ultra-permissive society. Have you changed enough for me to trust you?"

"I can go to Social Security," Joe growled, getting to his feet. So much for Nobby's bright idea!

"Sit down!"

Joe felt compelled to obey. There was hidden strength in this woman.

"We don't sponsor habitual criminals," Mrs. Hale told him. "Our aim is to give the first offender an opportunity to establish a working relationship with his fellow men. We have a strict rule – help once, no more."

"I'm not going back," Joe replied sourly.

"I should hope not. How much money do you have?"

He emptied his pockets, placing the meagre amount on her desk. Glancing at the pathetic result of his prison pay-out, she smiled scathingly. "Not much for what you've suffered, eh?"

"They haven't got unions in prison yet," he answered with a sneer.

"That's quite enough cheek," she snapped. Counting his cash she said; "That's grocery money, Joe. I have an arrangement with a landlady in Islington. She'll provide a room and breakfast. It's not a palace but you'll have a front door key and freedom to come and go as you please. "

"Thanks!" He sounded bitter. Nobby had given him such glowing accounts of this outfit's cash reserves and how they treated their clients generously.

"Your attitude leaves much to be desired. I suppose your old lag friend spun you a yarn about how soft we were..." Her gorgeous breasts flattened on the desk as she leant forward. "Joe, pay attention to me."

His eyes fastened on her breasts. His pulse quickened. She was a magnificent woman and frustration seethed like super-charged electrons inside him. "I am," he said truthfully.

She ignored the obvious. "I'm going to tell you a story, Joe," she said evenly. "My son lives in Canada. He served five years in Kingston there and got a loan from this society. With it he met a girl, got married and found a job. Today, thank God, he's an honest citizen and owns his home, a business and has two beautiful children. That's why I work here, Joe. If my boy could do it – so can you." Joe sat motionless. *Why did they have to pour on the soft soap*, he asked himself. He didn't believe her. This was a standard approach to someone fresh out of stir.

"You've got doubts?"

He shrugged. "That's not for me to say."

She opened her desk drawer and pushed three scraps of paper across to him. It took less than five seconds for his eyes to confirm the truth of her tale. The newspaper clipping had the name Hale in bold headlines. The society loan agreement photostat showed that Hale had been granted five hundred dollars repayable over a set period. The third item was a glowing account of John Hale opening a community centre which his prosperous company had seen fit to build for the town's youth.

"Satisfied, Joe?"

He pushed the material back to her. "Yes!"

"My son never had a decent thought in his head until he served time," she said. "I despaired of him but now..." and her eyes moistened in motherly pride. "He's justified the faith I've placed in him. I'm a sentimental fool, Joe. I know this will shock you – and the society. I'm going to give you a chit for twenty pounds. I advise spending it wisely. Take ten and get roaring drunk. Find a girl and take her home with you. Relieve yourself. But don't make a habit of it. Mrs. Malloy does not like her bathroom occupied by strange women every morning."

Joe felt strangely touched. This was against everything he had considered possible. He wanted the money. He wanted the society behind him. If his plans were ever to reach fruition stage he had to have the backing of a solid community agency. But Mrs. Hale was putting trust in him. Placing him in an invidious position. If he failed her... He mentally rejected her wiles. What the hell! He was Joe Hawkins. Not a Hale. This stupid game was meant to soften him. He would not yield.

"Try to better yourself, Joe" the woman said, writing the chit for his cash advance. "I believe there is good in everybody. I hope you won't let me down."

He accepted the chit and smiled. "I won't, Mrs. Hale."

Outside her office he breathed deeply. So much for that! The woman was a sucker for a hard luck story. Once his twenty vanished he could come back and beg for more. He would have a story to tell – all sobs and under-the-skin frustration!

*

Mrs. Malloy was short, fat and ugly. She spoke with a thick Dublin accent, and smelt of wash-tub detergent. Rubbing clean, almost raw hands on her apron, she stood in the doorway studying Joe as he eyed his room with candid disgust.

"Bhoyo," the Irish woman said, "forget your grand notions. This is Islington and the Society are paying for your keep. Back in the Auld Sod there are fine fellas wishing they could afford such luxuries. Take my Uncle Sean..." She sighed as if trying to find someone to do just that! "He lives in me mother's auld house with its roof falling in and the rats climbing into bed at night just to get warmth."

"Where's the loo?" Joe asked.

"A fine thing..." She said "thing" like it had no "h". "You're everything Mrs. Hale said you'd be." Her ugly features showed contempt. "You'll be wanting a key, no doubt?" She walked to the window, fluffed curtains to hide the solid brick wall a mere three feet away. A thin shaft of light edged into the narrow confines of Joe's "home" and served to highlight the shabby furnishings. "I'm Catholic," the woman said stridently. "I'm agin mortal sinning but Mrs. Hale knows better than I..." She shrugged as if to state where Mrs. Hale stood in her estimation. "There's an awful lot of terrible diseases in London today."

Joe grinned. The old biddy was trying to warn him against bringing home an "unclean" girl! Looking at her he wondered if any man had ever managed to get close to her soft-centre. She was ro-ly-poly in a most nauseous way. A man would have to be blind, drunk, desperate or very insensitive to take this one to bed.

"Patrick Kelly shares the toilet with you. He lives in the next room. You'll be wanting to meet the dear boy..."

Not me, Joe thought. *I'm not going to get tied-in with a bunch of booze artists from construction sites.*

He knew all about the Irish labouring types and how they roamed the streets before the pubs opened and how they sang their "rebel" songs with a skin-ful of booze making each and every one of them im-agine they could wipe the floor with all English in-habitants after the pubs closed. More than once his gang had waylaid a lone Irishman and beat the hell out of him. Just for kicks. Just to even the score, as Benny had once said.

"If my husband was still alive – bless his soul – he'd tell you a few truths," Mrs. Malloy remarked, retreating to the corridor outside Joe's room. "He spent sixteen years in prison!" She got uglier as frowns creased her blubbery face. "What a rascal he was, Joe... broke heads like skittles in an alley, he did. There wasn't a copper could tame my Mick."

"Charming," Joe allowed.

The woman scowled which only served to heighten her bushy eyebrows and those hard lines near her mouth. A discerning individual would have understood the terrible hardships which had produced such an unattractive female. Not Joe, though. He was filled with self-pity, and other people's problems washed off his uncaring hide.

Taking a Yale key from her apron, Mrs. Malloy said: "Breakfast is at seven-fifteen sharp."

"Seven-fifteen?" Joe wailed. Looking frantically around the sparse room he asked, "Where do I cook?"

"Not in here! You can use the kitchen anytime after twelve noon if you have to eat in. My other bhoyos don't do that." She sounded anxious to put him off cooking.

"I was told..."

"Mrs. Hale doesn't live here," the woman said firmly. "She's a lady. I'm not. Nor are my guests gentlemen." The point was made and she relented briefly with a quick smile.

Joe kept his retort to himself. It pleased him to have one thin-edge to wedge in Mrs. Hale's door. He could always complain that his cash did not stress to restaurant or cafe meals. Any excuse was valid under the circumstances. He could not continue to live in this worse mousetrap which Mrs. Malloy called a room. It was ten times more horrible than his room at home in Plaistow – and that was bad enough.

"I'll be looking for a job," Joe said, changing subjects. "In the city," he stressed emphatically. "I'll want a key to the post box..." He could see that locked cage attached to the letterbox downstairs.

"You'll get your letters at breakfast," the woman said menacingly.

"Why can't I have a key?"

Hands on wide hips she snapped: "'Cos nobody but me is allowed to sort the post. I don't tru..." She stopped and swung abruptly.

"You don't trust jailbirds," Joe finished.

She hesitated momentarily, and then continued down the corridor as if afraid to pursue this line of questioning.

What a bloody mess, Joe thought angrily. *It's as bad as prison. I'm trapped with nowhere to go!*

Closing his door, Joe examined the dingy room in detail. That brick wall hemmed him in as effectively as bars on a window. The tatty covers on the sagging bed were below standard issue even for the Scrubs. As for the small chest of drawers, the wardrobe and one tilted chair, they had come from Noah's Ark and had been junk before an elephant sat on the chair or tigers sharpened their tearing claws on the other two items. A threadbare carpet from an Honest Ed's bargain basement did little to cover dry rot floors. Wallpaper that was so faded to have lost its distinctive floral design completed the picture of misery.

"Chrissakes, this is hell!" Joe yelled at that brick wall.

The touch of folding money in his pocket drained some of his hate. Then, he swore aloud again. What woman, or girl, or even club hostess would come back to this... this... this stink-hole of an abode? He hurried to the bed and pressed down on its wilted mattress. The rusting groan of battered springs sent their squeaking lullaby through the house.

"That's bloody it!" Joe shouted. Rage boiled up inside him and he kicked the chair. Splintering wood confirmed his fears. It had been an *impossible* seat anyway!

Thrusting arms into his jacket, he stormed from the room. His feet sounded like tanks rumbling down an incline formed of loose shell. He tore past a startled Mrs. Malloy and slammed the front door. Anger made him unaware of the pretty girl in hot pants brushing past him as she fumbled for a key in her Indian-style fringed handbag. He could only visualise Mrs. Hale and hear her remark: "It's not a palace..." *Bloody right it isn't*, he thought. *It's a tragedy – a free prison for ex-cons to discover how society gave to those who had repaid their debts!*

*

"Here's your bloody money back," Joe snarled as the twenty quid skittered across her desk. A fiver floated on an isolated air-current and drifted unheeled to the office floor.

Bernice Hale smiled grimly. In all her experience she had never encountered such an irate young man nor had money thrown at her. Usually they came in with their hats in hand and begging in their weak eyes. But not Joe Hawkins. He was strong stuff.

"When you make out a report be sure and mention this," Joe growled, beginning to turn away.

"There won't be any report, Joe."

He halted in mid-step, stared at the woman facing him across the paper-littered desk.

"What is wrong, Joe?"

He leant on her desk, face twisted into a contorted mask of frustration. "Mrs. Malloy is an Irish pig and expects everybody to act like she was giving them the world on a silver platter."

Bernice smiled generously. "That's not bad for you, Joe," she said softly. "Your kind don't normally stoop to poetic expression."

"You're making a bloody fool of me," Joe rasped.

"I am not! Perhaps you haven't stopped to examine what changes prison has worked inside your mind, Joe. Perhaps you always had a brain which could cope with the finer things your environment did not encourage. Perhaps not. Anyway, your choice of words strike me as being a notch above those skinheads I have the dubious pleasure of assisting."

"I'm not a skinhead now," Joe said, remembering his determination to disassociate with a former existence. He had to play his cards with masterly skill. He could not relax one single second in front of this woman. So much depended on getting accepted; established in an organised society to which she belonged.

"You were one of the best..." and she laughed lightly, adding, "or worst."

"I was," Joe affirmed proudly.

"And?"

"I'm not going to stay at Mrs. Malloy's!"

"Why not?"

"God," he exploded, "Have you seen that dump?"

"Is it that bad?" she brushed a paperclip which had attached itself from a blouse button. His gaze automatically fastened on her breasts. Self-consciously she covered her treasure chest with a file.

Joe got the message. *She's bashful after all,* he thought. *She's a tease who can't go beyond a certain set point. Once a guy gets the upper hand she's putty.*

Bernice Hale quivered inwardly. She hoped Joe Hawkins had not noticed her infantile attempt to turn his masculine frustrations away from those abundant charms which, she knew only too well, excited less deprived males. In a way she detested her wonderful bosom. It was a target for lasciviousness, for speculation, for passes she did not want made. She could not, however, deny herself the pleasure of mental seduction. She was all woman. All female as Eve would have it. And in the knowledge of the exquisite power her chest measurements gave her she basked in either glory or torment.

Joe calculated his chances. She was more than twice his age but he'd heard that the old ones were the best. Who was it who'd said: They don't yell, they don't tell and by jove they don't swell? Could he make the grade? Or would that ruin his ambitions?

He decided to play safe and ignored those hormones demanding he capitalise on the woman's confusion.

"I'd rather be in jail than stay in that room, Mrs. Hale," he said with a measure of truth which lent sincerity to his voice.

Thankful for small mercies, Bernice Hale breathed easier and placed the file back on her desk. The moment of indecision had departed on

Adam-strength wings. Or the ones he wore before the apple was eaten! "I haven't personally visited Mrs. Malloy's establishment," she admitted. "One of my colleagues gave it a recommendation."

"He didn't look at *my* room."

"Nor have the experience of what happens to a man once those prison gates shut, eh?" She smiled to relax his tenseness. "Joe, tell me honestly – what did you dislike about Mrs. Malloy's place?"

He considered her question. The native cunning which had taken him to the top of a skinhead gang and brought him to that fragile pinnacle of success for those fleeting hours of glory came rushing to his rescue. He was totally incapable of matching intellectual fencing but he knew when to duck and weave once fists started to fly. And this was street warfare. He was the underdog, the underprivileged. She the power, the rich, the one able to take away or give freely.

"I'm trying to get a decent job, Mrs. Hale. I need an address managers will respect. I need some comforts if I am to work my way to the top – not broken chairs and a bed that belongs in a dump."

She nodded thoughtfully. "Can you find a place yourself?"

"Yes!" He shouted the word, anxious now.

"I'm going to go overboard for you, Joe," she said falteringly, not quite satisfied with her decision yet realising it was all she could do under the given circumstances. "I'll advance you a loan. You'll have to sign for it though," she added pointedly.

"That's okay, Mrs. Hale. I'll refund it when I get work." He would have promised the moon plus a shilling for cash.

"Mark my words, Joe – this is your lot. Blow the cash and you're out in the cold."

"I won't let you down, Mrs. Hale," Joe said with mental fingers crossed she wouldn't change her mind at this stage.

She drew a chit across the desk, glanced at his face before writing figures. She could not know that Joe Hawkins was an actor. That the face he presented for her approval was but a facade behind which woodworm worked its nefarious quest.

"Sign here, Joe."

Catching himself in the nick of time, Joe scrawled his brash signature. Fifty quid! No interest. No repayment date. Just a name and the money was his...

"Let me know where you are staying," she said softly. "I'll want to visit you there."

He killed a thrill. If she came to his room he'd try her, for sure. Mother-age or not, she was everything a virile hunk of manhood dreamed about. He had seen her in a dozen erotic nights as moonlight filtered through those prison bars. Her, or a thousand panting females of all ages, all colours, all sizes. His face withheld the untold pleasures his mind conjured up and he kept his voice level as he said: "Thanks Mrs. Hale. I won't let you down."

"You said that once before." She laughed, handing him the initialled chit. "Joe Hawkins, you're a challenge for me. You're so like my son…" Tears moistened her eyes. She forced herself to regain control. "Remember where he went once he discovered that people are not all bad. Good luck in your job, Joe…" Her hand reached out and she stood – an attractive woman in her prime – as the lusting young man standing on the threshold of life let her warmth briefly touch his hard, unyielding, unsympathetic palm.

CHAPTER THREE

JOHN MATSON had once been a chippie working the London stage but opportunity and an inborn greed which knew no morality had taken the ex-carpenter to heights which only those owning a Rolls could ever aspire to reach. Thanks to a steal-happy thinking process and a desire to become larger than life had ever intended him to be, Matson was now perched on the apex of an expanding pornographic empire effectively covered by an equally profitable florist chain.

The men Matson employed called him "God" – Joe Hawkins included. Matson could do no wrong, or so the tall, broad-shouldered golfer liked to believe. The castle in Spain, the residence in St. John's

Wood, the estate down in Surrey were all tokens of Matson's income-tax-free rise to fame.

That the days of wine, women and illegal takes were fast approaching their end did not unduly worry the Matsons of Soho. They had made their killings. They had the wealth supplied by suckers seeking second-hand thrills from books, dirty pictures and available women. In his rise to the stratosphere Matson had used, abused, and thrown aside a string of excellent writers, photographers, models. He had made enemies but he was backed by heavies and a Vice Squad accepting his payola to such an extent that anyone daring to voice a protest found himself being turned over and in possession of damaging material. That was the way Matson operated and Joe felt himself unique when he suddenly quit.

He figured he got out just in the nick of time. Matson had not taken him on from sympathy. Matson had plans for Joe – another stretch inside, no doubt. In those three weeks working for Soho's undisputed kingpin, Joe had found himself being set up like a pin in a ten-pin alley. Ready to be bowled over at the first signs of trouble.

The second job proved less dangerous, more boring. It lasted exactly ten days – including a weekend off. Being a so-called accountant for a firm publishing sex manuals did not strike Joe as a route to the upper-bracket income levels. He quit, and appealed to Bernice Hale for help in securing a "decent" position with a City firm – without the necessity of explaining what he had done with eighteen months less remission.

The excuse offered by a believing Mrs. Hale appealed to Joe. Studies took full time occupation. One could not work as a coal-heaver and make the grade in accountancy. So, Joe applied for jobs armed with knowledge and a lie tailor-made to suit a discerning, inquisitive employer.

Stanman, Pierce & Solley had a reputation for integrity, a credit rating up to the moon orbit class, and a vacancy for a junior clerk which Joe landed. Mr. Pierce interviewed Joe and treated his prospective employee to a searching enquiry.

"Mr. Hawkins, let me say you have admirable qualifications," the dry starched City-man said as he examined the results of Joe's standard test. Rubbing his cold hands on a linen handkerchief, Pierce carefully replaced the folded emblem of his manicure-clean life in a breast pocket and gazed at Joe through rimless spectacles. "You have managed to accumulate a remarkable total of points. Your chief ability appears to be speed – which is precisely what is required in this position."

Joe congratulated himself silently. Short cuts had always been his forte. The prison accountant had shown him several tricks and he had latched onto each with an alacrity which had astounded the once-top embezzler.

Long, lean, lonely Pierce continued: "Where did you learn to calculate percentages to such perfection, Mr. Hawkins?"

Joe smirked behind a hand ostensibly covering a nasty cough. Lonely Pierce! That suited the musty old bastard. No sane woman would let this parchment-crackling flesh into her bed. Removing his hand, Joe said: "I attended private lessons from a friend of the family. A chartered accountant, you know!"

Pierce was impressed. He positively beamed. "Excellent, young man. All too few of your generation bother to take instructions from the elders. Have you ever had a job before?"

Joe hesitated. "Yes, sir."

"With whom?" A pen poised ready to make notations.

He's after references, Joe thought quickly.

"Come, boy – with whom?" Pierce demanded slightly agitated.

"Er..." Joe swallowed, and confessed with Oscar-winning embarrassment, "I am not from a middle-class family, sir. I come from poor people. I worked with a coal merchant before I decided to better myself."

"Ahhhh!" Pierce bestowed a generous smile on his "find". "Rags to riches, eh? A modern progression, lad. Oh, well – we must accept your ability. How does eleven pounds a week sound?"

Rotten! Joe thought instantly. To Pierce he smiled and said: "Wonderful, sir."

"Settled!" The man rose to his creaking feet, began to extend a hand and withdrew it immediately. "Hawkins..." Joe noted the dropped Mr. or the familiar Joe. "We are short-handed. Can you start tomorrow?"

Tomorrow was Wednesday – middle of the pay week. Joe mulled over the problem of his next loan from the society. If he played his cards right he might just scrape home with an additional tenner.

"When do I get my first pay, sir?" He cursed himself at once when Pierce raised a scanty eyebrow and fixed him with an accusing stare. "I hate to appear anxious, sir, but there are circumstances which I have not mentioned."

"Like what, Hawkins?"

"Well, sir..." Joe thought fast and found a solution. "I mentioned being from a poor family. My parents do not understand why I should want to better myself, sir. I have a small flat but I'm hard-pressed for the..." He had started to say "ready" but quickly changed this to, "money to pay my landlady. I'm alright until Saturday, sir..."

Pierce smiled until his dry lips started to crack. "I like your spirit, Hawkins. It isn't every day we come face to face with a lad willing to sacrifice home and family in an endeavour to rise above lower class graveyards. I'll personally make arrangements for you to draw a full week's pay this Friday. Is that enough?"

"Thank you, sir!" Joe sounded so convincing he began to wonder if, somewhere along the line, he had actually begun to *think* like these stupid creeps.

"Right, Hawkins. See you in the morning at nine-thirty." Pierce dismissed his "help" with an imperious gesture and sank back into his leather-cushioned chair. The sigh of relief spoke volumes as those long, skin-over-bones fingers began rifling through stock market tapes.

Leaving the musty office with its leather-bound tomes and its legalistic, money-making atmosphere, Joe felt the world had for once returned him a debt. He had been long overdue recognition. He might have preferred to be known as "king of skinheads" but by his reckoning, this set-up would return more authority and more eventual glory than all the commands ever granted to a skinhead leader.

Those silly bastards beating their heads against stone walls are trash compared to what I'll be once I'm established, he thought as he walked through the offices of his employers. *Look at those girls in their mini-skirts and hot pants. They're ripe for someone like me. And as for Pierce – crissakes, I could steal him blind and he'd never suspect.*

CHAPTER FOUR

IT WAS OPENING time and Joe hurried along the Bayswater Road. He felt thirsty – and randy. Maybe he could find a girl in the pub: one willing to come back to his flatlet and spend this Sunday afternoon in his company. He had no worries now about bringing anyone to where he called home. Although he lived on the third floor, the entire building was nicely decorated and modest carpets covered every flight of stairs so that passing feet did not disturb the tenants.

His own room reflected some of the large house's former glory – decorated ceilings with sunburst plaster-work round the hanging, shaded light, doors dating back to a period just after Regency. Joe did not know about such refinements. He knew that he liked the place and there his information ended. Abruptly. Sadly.

He shared a toilet and bath with two other flatlets but he had cooking facilities, a washbasin, a large closet which doubled as a kitchen-cum-storage room, and a spacious bedsitter containing twin comfortable beds, a dressing table, chest of drawers, armchair in fresh upholstery and three ordinary chairs for eating at the gate-leg table. The room was carpeted, clean and serviced once a week. He had purchased one of those plastic wardrobes for his coat and suit – singular since he had not bothered to visit his real home since walking free from the Scrubs. *To hell with the old man, he kept thinking. To hell with the old woman. Not even if I'm starving would I call on them for help.*

Artists were displaying their multi-hued wares across the Bayswater Road as he approached the pub. Dozens of gawking tourists strolled aimlessly past the over-priced paintings and miscellaneous artifacts. Behind the railings – seen through gaps left as an occasional painting was sold for a knockdown "bargain" – the green grass of the park looked slightly artificial in this concrete jungle that was seething, bustling, swinging London.

In his pin-stripe suit and clean white shirt with his conservative tie clipped in place by a Stratton gold pin, Joe felt quite the City gent. *Funny,* he mused, *how clothes change a guy's outlook.*

He could remember those far-off days when he felt ten foot tall dressed in bovver boots, union shirt and tight trousers with the loud braces boldly showing. He could touch his hair and recall the pride of a skinhead cut. *Recall!* His hair was growing now. In another month or two it would be suede... in between being a skinhead and being what the Establishment liked to call normal styling. *Suede* – smooth, elite, expensive.

He smiled to himself as he entered the pub. That was his new image. Suedehead – a smoothie, one of the elite now, and with expensive tastes and ambitions.

Thumbs behind his lapels, he straightened his jacket and marched to the crowded bar. A huge roast beef stared back at him amid a variety of pickles, salads and other inviting snacks. He was hungry but he dared not spend on food. Mrs. Hale had paid for the suit (an extra loan once he got his City job) but the well was drying up. The society did not have inexhaustible funds for Joe Hawkins, apparently. Not that he minded. He made out okay. He was in for seventy-five quid. On his signature only. And unknown to the ever-smiling, ever-helpful Mrs. Hale he was working the dodge with Social Security too. Life was great. Terrific. Everybody paid for his pleasure. To a degree...

Mentally he calculated what was left in his wallet. Certainly not more than fifteen nicker. Not less than twelve. He had to buy smokes – a decent brand now he was a *member* of Stanman, Pierce and Solley. He could still drink pints of wallop but he enjoyed putting on the dog and having shorts with soda. And they cost a packet! If he met a dolly-bird she would probably insist on some exotic concoction so... He fought back the desire to have a beef sandwich with a side salad and settled for a hot sausage on a cocktail stick with Seagram's Hundred Pipers splashed lightly with soda.

Squeezing into a seat between a man-wife duo and two hot-panted dolly-birds he eyed what the girls were drinking before unleashing a smile in their combined direction. He could afford to pay for a few rounds. After all, it wasn't every day a bloke got to grips with birds who preferred milds and bitter to shorts.

He munched the sausage like it was hors d'oeuvres, sipped his drink in leisurely fashion. He wanted to knock it back, order another, but discretion was the pocket dictate. He let the girls know he was interested without ever stepping on toes. The old methods did not work in this new atmosphere. Anyway the man-wife team were furtively watching him as if expecting a rapist to emerge from inside that pin-stripe suit at any second.

One girl – smallish, pretty, wearing her hair in a huge knot at the back – laughed as she finished her drink. "How about another Sandra?" she asked her companion.

Sandra was taller, leaner, less inclined to toss glances in Joe's direction. She was also in Joe's opinion, a spoilt brat and decidedly trying to put a wet blanket on her mate's fun. "Not for me," she pebble-mouthed. "I find this crowd disgustingly cheap."

Oh, la-la, Joe thought. *What the hell would she think if she had to drink with his old crowd down in East Ham?*

"Sandra! That's awful... keep your voice low!"

Sandra giggled and sipped what remained of her pint. "Sorry if I embarrass you, Lois."

"You're deliberately trying to make me feel small."

"You are small," Sandra replied cattily.

The man and woman quickly finished their drinks and departed. Leaning across the table Joe said: "You're not that small, Lois."

The girl avoided a direct confrontation with Joe's hot eyes. Lowering her head she softly said: "Sandra believes every woman worth anything should be five-eight."

"Not true," Joe told her. "Would you like a drink — one on me?"

Lois nodded quickly.

"Sandra?"

The taller girl shook her head defiantly, then got to her feet leaving an inch of beer in her glass. "No thanks. I'm going. Are you staying, Lois?"

Joe tensed expectantly.

"I think I shall…"

Joe got to his feet with alacrity. "What'll it be, Lois?"

"Would you mind awfully if I switched to the same as you?"

He forced a brave smile. This wasn't what he had figured but… "It's Scotch and soda," he warned.

"Lovely. I often sneak a sample of daddy's scotch."

"Large?" Joe cursed his tongue immediately.

"Thanks – yes!"

As Sandra took a dignified exit Joe got the barmaid's attention and ordered large Hundred Pipers for two. He did not think to bring the soda back to Lois so she could fix her own mixture. Instead, he liberally splashed both drinks and went back like an uncrowned monarch about to dispense favours to a loyal subject. He had a lot to learn though the lesson was not imminent.

Lois smiled, sipped her drink after a murmured, "cheers", and kept her gaze alerted.

"I haven't seen you here before," Joe said conversationally as if he was a regular. In fact, he had been inside this particular pub but only once before. The first night he took his flatlet.

"That wouldn't surprise me," the girl remarked. "I live on the other side of the park."

Joe stiffened. Her very word "other" made his side seem vile, vulgar, violent. He would have to be careful with this one. She came from a society family, he was sure. The "daddy" bit and Sandra's down-the-nose attitude spoke of slumming.

"I've only moved in myself," Joe said to lessen the antagonism between their classes.

She appeared interested. "Oh, where did you live previously?"

"Actually," he lied effectively, "I'm a roving bod." He was getting quite expert at inventing backgrounds and denying his past.

"That must be fun." She looked straight into his eyes and blushed a little.

"Fun is not being alone all the time," Joe said to open the conversation.

"I'm Lois, as you know. What's your name?"

"Joe..." He balked at the Hawkins. That sounded common!

A fat girl accompanied by a slender man slid into the unoccupied seats. "What'll you have, ducks?" The man asked.

"Pint of cider," fatso said eagerly.

Joe shuddered. Why did *they* have to invade his upper-class territory.

"I like this Scotch. What brand is it?" Lois asked as if the rest of the world did not exist at that precise moment.

"Seagram's Hundred Pipers. Quite new, I understand."

"Seagram's... are they the people who make Canadian rye?"

Joe wasn't sure but he tried to appear knowledgeable. "Why yes, they are."

Lois glanced at the fat girl, smiled at Joe. "Crowded isn't it?"

You little viper, Joe thought. "Sunday..." he explained.

"I'm hungry – are you?"

I'm bloody starving, his mind screamed.

"Finish your drink. We'll find a c..." He almost said "caff". "A cosy restaurant," he finished lamely. It was a bloody effort dealing with these snooty bitches. And trying to rise above his skinhead, East End background.

"There's a smashing one across the park."

There would be! He nodded thoughtfully. "Anything you want, Lois." *Within reason and my pocket-book.*

*

Immediately he saw the facade and the saw-dust floor he knew this was more than he had expected. And he had allowed for a costly interlude before bringing her back through the park and into his bed.

Once inside, however, he felt better. The menu did not read like the national debt. It was reasonable. He'd have to remember Flanagan's. Posh, a throw-back to Edwardian times and the right type of atmosphere to make any reluctant virgin say "yes" without hesitation. He felt better, more inclined to splurge. Soon, he'd have money to do those things he had always thought were his due. He'd be like the stars in a black void as gazed upon by astronauts – a millionaire. Hawkins would not be a surname to feel ashamed of then. It would be a title almost.

Thrusting aside his daydreams he concentrated on the menu.

"I'll have Royal Game Pie," Lois declared.

"Me, too." He dropped the menu.

"With Spotted Dick?"

"Naturally!" He feigned aloofness, not bothering to cast a second glance at the menu. The act went over excellently, he thought, as her eyes shone enthusiastically.

"Shall we have something to drink?"

He swore inwardly. This was the test. He knew absolutely nothing about wines, about correct procedures. Beer was fine with chicken according to him, according to his old man.

"You must have a favourite," he suggested.

Lois smiled thanks. "I enjoy Sauterne."

The waitress nodded approval. Joe puffed out his chest. "A bottle of Sauterne, miss."

What the hell is Sauterne? he asked mentally. He had never tasted the drink. But never!

Waiting for their order, Joe studied Lois. She was more than pretty. She was beautiful. She had large, luminous blue eyes and the way her chestnut coloured hair was gathered into that backknot made her face definitely exciting. Her figure left much to be praised, nothing to be desired. She had firm, high breasts; lovely legs admirably displayed in those velvety-green hotpants. Her skin was pure satin – smooth, blemishless, so naturally untouched.

"What do you do for a living?" she asked.

"I'm *with* Stanman, Pierce & Solley, stockbrokers."

Mrs. Hale had been adamant. She had insisted he refer to his position as being *with* the company. Not merely a junior clerk working *for* them.

Lois's blue eyes enlarged into liquid pools expressing her joy at finding "one of her own" on the Bayswater side of the park. "Fascinating, Joseph," she said.

The hell with you, bitch! Joe thought. *Joseph, indeed! Never!*

"The name is Joe," he said tightly.

She did not catch his tension. "I think that Joseph is a marvellous name. Much better than Joe."

"I'm Joe," he said viciously.

She began to worry. This wasn't a boy willing to please a girl's preference for a name. This was a stubborn man thrusting his opinionated self down a woman's throat. The arrival of the waitress saved her from an argument. She watched carefully as Joe quickly caught onto his duty and sampled the wine. He nodded, much too soon. *He isn't accustomed to this*, she thought.

Once – it had seemed like eons ago – Joe had read a book where the private eye had sampled wine and expressed his opinions on its merits. He saw those lines now and said: "A good year. Very palatable."

Lois frowned. Was she wrong? He sounded as if he knew...

*

"Shall we take a stroll around the park?"

Joe champed at the bit. The meal had been near disaster but by watching how she handled her knife and fork he had managed to avoid total disgrace. That time when a slice of pie had fallen from his fork had almost undone all he had hoped to achieve. Luckily, Lois had been lost in her flavour buds and listening to the conversation from the next table.

"Across the park," he said deliberately.

Her hand briefly touched his. "You're trying to compromise me, Joseph."

"Can't you do what I ask?" he requested pleadingly.

"What's that?"

"Call me plain Joe."

She laughed and concentrated on ducks floating lazily on placid waters. Their outrageously coloured feathers contrasted sharply with the brownishness of polluted, weed dank liquid.

"Do you have a job?" Joe asked finally. He was fast approaching tongue-tied frustration. If he did not have to keep being something he was not there were a dozen topics he could talk about. He'd have enjoyed discussing the merits of West Ham or Chelsea or Arsenal's chance of pulling off the "double". He could have spoken about the days when he ruled a gang with an iron hand and took those girls he liked with the simplicity of a stallion servicing a sprightly mare. But that was the past. His present image demanded less crudity, more gentility – and it was eating at his bone marrow at an alarming rate.

"A job?" She stared at him, trying hard not to show disgust. "Not a job, Jos... *Joe*! I am a partner in a boutique daddy bought for us."

"Us?" That gave him a new line.

"Sandra..."

"She's not your type," he said firmly.

"She's a bloody good saleswoman."

Joe smiled. So she swore on occasion. That would make it easier when he slipped back into the old mould.

They were now at the Bayswater Road with the pub to their right, crowds everywhere as the afternoon rush for bargain oils got under way. Artists no longer sat in their parked cars but mingled with the outspoken tourists and tried to cadge a quick sale once they heard a favourable comment on a specific work.

Joe had not experienced this seemingly positive urge to own an original oil but then, Joe Hawkins came from a home which had not been noted for its cultural belongings. The closest his family ever came to brushing against creative talent was the infrequent romance story borrowed from the public library and even that was usually a lesser work by a sausage-machine writer. Anything deep would have sailed above the heads of his parents. One head for two... Funny how he always thought of mother and father as a single unit! Perhaps it came from his own detachment from them both.

"I bought a landscape here once," Lois remarked acidly as he took her hand. She did not like having people guide her across busy streets. Without appearing to tear herself away she skillfully manoeuvred free and darted between moving vehicles until she stood waiting for her escort as he struggled with the traffic alone.

"You could get killed doing that," Joe panted as he joined her.

"If I do it shall be my fault, nobody else's," she replied with characteristic stubbornness.

Joe didn't quite know what to make of the girl. She had seemed docile, ready to be shaped for his passion. Now, he wasn't so certain. She had an iron will and a determination that society background and money in the bank made all the more frightening. He admitted that women like her scared the hell out of him. He preferred the little tarts utterly dependant on their menfolk. With them a man could get what he wanted without the bother of battling for mental supremacy.

"My place is along here," Joe pointed in the general direction of Devonshire Terrace.

Her face expressed concern. "A room?"

"A flatlet."

"Is there a difference?" she asked snootily.

God, I'd like to smack her ass, Joe thought.

"I'm not sure this is wise," Lois said, holding back at the corner.

"Look," Joe said in exasperation, "I'm not going to rape you."

"Bloody right you're not. I'm a virgin!"

"You mean...?" Joe asked in amazement.

"I've never been to bed with a chap!"

"S'truth!"

"Sorry you've spent money on me now?" the girl asked with a touch of sarcasm.

"Not at all." Joe attempted to put on a brave front. He cursed inwardly. Just his rotten luck. Of all the birds frequenting pubs he had to pick the only virgin left in the Bayswater district.

"You expected me to undress for you, though."

He nodded. The truth could not hurt. "Why not?"

"It's not being seen naked, Joe. It's what nudity arouses I worry about."

"Are you afraid to make love then?" He was getting lost in the quagmire of her purity.

"Yes – I suppose I am. One hears so much about venereal diseases these days."

"I haven't anything wrong with me," he said quickly.

"You may not have, Joe – but there's no medical certificate to say a doctor has examined you this morning."

"Damn! I'll wear..."

"Sorry. Not today, Joe."

"Don't you want to see my flatlet?"

"Can you promise not to start mucking around with me?"

"Yeah!"

"If you do I shall scream," she threatened.

Joe felt defeat heavy on his urges. He had gone too far to turn back. So what if she didn't let him.

He'd scheme for the future. He badly wanted to bed her. A day, or two would still taste as sweet. If he played his cards right she would weaken until she begged him to strip off her garments and treat her as he had all those others.

"Lois, I promise there won't be any nonsense today. Okay?"

She took his arm, felt the hard muscles ripple. She liked Joe, wished there was some method for sharing a mental passion without the absolute necessity of physical contact between bodies.

"I'll bet lots of guys have tried to get you into bed," Joe said with a grin. He had decided on his campaign. Talk about love-making. Get her so excited at the prospect of being naked in his arms that she would be unable, unwilling to forego the ultimate pleasure when he made his big play.

He was still promoting verbal emotion as they climbed the stairs to his room...

CHAPTER FIVE

ENTERING THE offices of Stanman, Pierce & Solley the following morning, Joe became immediately aware of a nervous silence. Three girls with heads together suddenly stopped chatting and gazed at him coldly. A young man carrying a tray full of letters already opened, briefly halted in mid-step before shrugging a casual welcome as he pushed into an inner office. In a far corner of the main reception area a balding, aged man rose to his feet and motioned for Joe to approach him.

"I'm Totter," the man said when Joe was a few feet away. "You'll be working directly under my supervision. Remove your coat, lad. We begin promptly at nine here."

Joe slowly took his coat off, wishing he could tell this grim-faced old bastard where to stick his promptness. Inside the space of two minutes he was already sorry he had taken Pierce's job. He had an idea there would be no joy working for this firm.

"I understand from Mr. Pierce you've never been engaged in stockbroking before," Totter said, not bothering to show Joe where the cloakroom was. "We demand a high standard..."

"Do I drop it on the floor?" Joe asked sarcastically, gesturing with his coat.

Totter glared. "Your attitude is abominable, lad."

"Sorry, sir!" Joe compelled himself to make the apology and call this man sir.

"I should think so. Hang it on that peg." Totter pointed firmly at a row of pegs holding a variety of male and female coats, umbrellas and shopping bags. A nearby hat rack held a collection of spotless bowlers and one lonely fedora. Joe wondered which member of staff dared to go against the grain and come to work sporting a *normal* hat. He would make it his business to become acquainted with the rebel.

Carefully, Joe hung his Crombie, brushing a speck from the sheening velvet collar and returned to face the indignant Totter.

"You will, I presume, wear a hat tomorrow?"

Joe shook with silent laughter. This could be fun. He would make it his business to rile the old bastard at every opportunity. The man was a granny – one of those male wonders married to a position. Joe doubted if he had ever known the exquisite thrill of belonging to the human race, of sharing passions with a woman.

"I asked you a question, lad," Trotter said.

"I suppose so, sir," Joe replied lightly. "Now where do I start?"

"Take this ledger into Mr. Solley's office and have him sign the last page."

"Which one is Solley's?"

"Mr. Solley to you, lad!"

"Which one, sir?" Joe ignored the correction.

Totter pointed again. Following the long, almost skinless finger, Joe entered a sumptuous room containing a massive desk, a teleprinter machine, a well-stocked bar, several comfortable leather chairs and shelves lined with large bound books. Although it was relatively warm outdoors, a small fire burned in an Adam grate immediately behind the huge man seated at the desk. Lifting a shaggy head, the man stared at Joe quizzically; allowing a flicker of a smile to soften his lined features.

"Mr. Totter wants your signature, Mr. Solley." He set the ledger on the desk and stood back waiting.

"You're new," Solley said with a resonant voice.

"I started this morning."

"Having trouble with our Totter, eh?"

Joe liked the other. He grinned. "A bit."

"We all have problems with old Totter. Be kind to him, boy. He's a genius with figures and we couldn't afford to lose him." It was a gentle way of warning Joe whose services could be under the hammer should trouble arise.

Flourishing a pen, Solley made a hasty assessment of the figures prepared for his signature, and scribbled his name right across the page. That done, he closed the book and pushed it across the desk. "Are you a football fan?" he asked.

"Yes, sir!" Joe rose to the question happily.

"Like a couple of tickets for Saturday's match?"

"Which team?"

Solley grinned. "Tottenham. Is something wrong?"

"Those f..." Joe lapsed into silence, face tense. It had been a near thing. He did not imagine *Mister* Stockbroker Solley swore as expertly as he could.

"Those what?" Solley asked, bending over the desk with hands clasped.

"Fools," Joe replied lamely. "I'm..." he thought fast. He couldn't say West Ham and deny all knowledge of the East End. Chelsea went against the grain, just as Spurs did. "I'm an Arsenal supporter myself."

"One man's meat," the man laughed as he reached inside his immaculate jacket. "Here – have all the fun of watching next year's champs." Two tickets floated down on to the desk.

Joe picked them up. "Thanks Mr. Solley. Don't the other guys watch soccer?"

"I'm afraid they consider me a traitor to rugby. What's your name, son?"

"Joe Hawkins."

"Well, Joe – don't let me hear you refer to our staff as guys. They are chaps, or fellows, or if the mood merits, rotten bastards. Never guys."

"I'll remember, sir."

"Do you wear a hat, Joe?"

"I shall, sir."

"Make it a bowler. I alone break the rules." He chuckled. "I look damned silly in a hard hat. That's all, boy. Back to the grind."

As he took his departure, Joe dropped the notion of cultivating the fedora owner. He thought Solley a decent bloke but hardly one to call "mate" as they swilled pints together. It was a perk getting the football tickets but not one to make him a solid citizen in anybody's eyes yet. Given time, he'd qualify for a higher position. The burning ambition to succeed was in him. All he needed was a chance for some fast lolly, a few birds to make his evenings worthwhile and a gang to bolster his ego. Not a bunch of yobbos. That was out. He wanted some "chaps" willing to commit mayhem under cover of respectability.

*

He was eighteen, tall, not bad looking. In his City suit, the Crombie coat with velvet collar, his furled umbrella and the new bowler perched cockily on his head, he was enough to make silly little birds take a second glance and get their hormones working overtime. Every night as he travelled home from Bank on the Central Line he could feel those hot, passionate eyes seek to catch his attention. It was some strain to ignore each and every one of them but somehow he managed. Lois first – then the world of pearl-glistening oyster-birds.

Even Totter had praised him that day which was a change. Usually the old bastard screamed and threatened when he made the slightest mistake. But today Joe had reaped rewards for spotting a glaring error in Totter's addition. Something was worrying the old man. Joe could tell. More than once he'd caught Totter peering out of the window with a vacant expression on his tight, parchment face. The fact that the firm's oldest, most trusted employee had faltered proved Joe's suspicions – Totter was having family troubles. Still, it was Friday and the office could go to hell until Monday.

Brushing a loose hair from his forehead, he caught sight of the man seated across from him. There was that pathetic desire of the homosexual about to smile in search of a mutually inclined soul about the man. Joe froze. If he made the slightest...

He unfroze quickly! Deliberately he yawned and smiled at nothing.

The man inched forward on his seat, returning what he thought was Joe's opening gambit.

The dirty old bastard, Joe thought. *He looks like he has a fat wallet. I wonder...* At Holborn the train stopped and another seething mass of humanity shoved and kicked into the carriage. The man rose, giving his seat to a young girl. Joe wanted to laugh. He knew what came next was "standard procedure" and waited until the man sidled to a strap hanger directly in front of him. Their knees touched, pressure increased.

"Sorry..." the man said with an almost feminine voice.

Joe gestured expansively. "That's alright."

The knee assaulted anew.

God, it's too easy, Joe told himself.

By Lancaster Gate the man was mentally raping Joe. There was no pretence now. It was a plain case of "wait until we get to my place, young lad".

At Queensway the man smiled and said softly: "This is where I live," and headed for the open door. Joe followed.

On the station platform the man took Joe's hand and squeezed.

"Do you...?"

"Anything," Joe replied with a return squeeze.

Joe wanted to vomit. As a skinhead he would have kicked the bastard in the balls and hoped to ruin his love life forever. But that was not how the new Joe Hawkins operated. Not how a neophyte suedehead got the wherewithal to continue as a member of a decent community. The take home pay from Stanman, Pierce & Solley did not begin to pay for his clothes, flatlet, food or entertainment. It was a hand-out to keep him fed and sheltered so that he could slave his guts out preparing statements and tax returns. Only that.

"I'll follow you," Joe said in a whisper. "I wouldn't want my neighbours to know…"

The man trembled. "Yes… yes, of course. That will be better for both of us. I live with Auntie… she's a darling but so possessive. She's away in Bristol for the weekend, you know!"

Joe didn't know but he nodded sagely. "Lead on, McBent."

The queer giggled girlishly and hurried along the platform. He was delighted, intent on a weekend spent in this young man's company.

Poor Auntie, Joe thought. *She must be a right bitch. Stupid, to boot. Anyone could tell he's round the twist.*

Surprisingly, the man guided Joe into one of those sedate, family hotels catering for permanent guests along the Bayswater Road. Once inside the suite of rooms allocated to Auntie and her bent nephew, Joe found himself confronted by blowing curtains as a breeze wafted in from the park. One glance and Joe knew the bastard was well-heeled. Antiques galore dotted Victorian what-nots and Georgian sideboards, and the silverware displayed on a dresser had cost a bomb way back when men toiled for a pittance per year.

"Take your coat off and relax," the queer said. "Like a drink first?"

Joe kept his coat securely buttoned. "How much, pal?"

The man paled perceptively. "What?"

"How much?" Joe repeated.

"I... I thought..."

"Free love?"

"Er, yes."

"Sorry, luv – good times come expensive these days."

"Would five...?"

"I'm going!" Joe announced indignantly.

"Ten?"

"That depends on what you want, doesn't it?"

The man's fingers shook as he extracted a wallet from inside his jacket. He peeled off five fivers and offered them. Joe caught sight of tens and at least one twenty. Greed gnawed at his guts.

"I'll have a large Scotch first," Joe announced, ignoring the money in that trembling, eager hand.

"Certainly..." The twenty-five pounds lay on a sofa within reach as the man hurried to a cabinet and began pouring drinks.

Two drinks and then, Joe thought.

"You're sweet," the man said as he handed Joe the glass.

"You're dirty," Joe laughed.

"Ohhh," the man laughed, too.

"Don't you like it with women?"

A shudder raced through the man. "No! They're... they're–"

"Like Auntie?" Joe suggested.

The man's eyes narrowed. "Are you one of us?"

Joe finished his drink. He'd overplayed his hand. The next glass of Scotch would have to be taken, like this creep and his loot.

"You're not..."the man started to say.

Joe's toe caught him in the groin and, as the pathetic creature staggered back with hands flying to protect – and sympathise with – his injured manhood, Joe followed in with hard fist. All the fury, all the hatred went into those vicious fists. Slowly, steadily, Joe beat the man to a pulp until his whimpering ceased and he collapsed to the floor.

Working fast, Joe counted what was in the wallet. One hundred and seven pounds. Not bad! Leaving the man where he had fallen, Joe searched the entire suite. He discovered another thirty six quid and a small suitcase which he packed with silver objects he reckoned would bring the highest resale price.

As a final gesture of defiance he stole the man's Omega watch, his solid gold cuff links and tie clip and added insult to injury by appropriating a Sanyo global transistor radio which he liked.

A groan echoed from the depths of the man's chest.

"Tough luck, mate," Joe snarled and grinding his heel where the pain would be most acute, he bent over and belted the man again. "That'll keep you cold until I make my getaway..."

CHAPTER SIX

"This is The Voice of America coming to you..."

Joe smiled indulgently and flipped through the pages of his magazine. He adored *his* Sanyo transistor. With it he could catch up on world trends and dazzle his fellow workers with his global knowledge. He required very little sleep. After all, he was young, strong and healthy. Not one of those crusty old men the firm usually employed. If he got to sleep by three a.m. he could rise by seven-thirty and be at his desk promptly at nine – something Mr. Totter insisted upon each and every morning of the week.

Turning the page, an article caught his eye. The radio was forgotten now.

"Suedeheads," the article said, "are difficult to define. They belong to no known bands nor do they amalgamate into gangs as their skinhead predecessors did. They are an enigma. An anti-social anti-everything conglomerate affecting status as their protective cover whilst engaging in nefarious pursuits more savage, more brutal than other cultists we have seen rise – and fall in this past decade."

"*...and now, the Glen Miller sound. Little Brown Jug has been requested by Staff-Sergeant Harry Carr from Munich...*"

Joe dropped the magazine to the floor and fiddled with the dial.

"*Ici...*"

He turned on. Foreign language programmes gave him a headache trying to cut through nasalness and unintelligible garble.

"*...Berlin: British troops staged a three day exercise to prove their readiness for any Soviet sneak attack...*"

He whirled the dial viciously and then switched to another wavelength.

The suedehead article was a magnet he could not fight against. His fingers playfully shifted the selector to a music programme and dropped away. He picked up the magazine again and got involved in it to such an extent he did not hear the foreign disc-jockey's voice gutturally berate the latest offering from an established English pop group.

"...and suedeheads have been known to use their umbrellas as weapons..."

Joe glanced across the room at his furled umbrella.

"Many adherents of this strange, loosely-joined cult have resorted to sharpening their umbrella tips..."

Immediately, Joe saw the possibilities. What a beautiful cover-up! Leaving the radio blaring on its alien station, he got his umbrella and examined the tip. By removing the metal end, he could easily have the staff fashioned into a lethal weapon. A dab of black paint would effectively camouflage his handiwork...

*

Being a suedehead with its loose links appealed to the new Joe Hawkins. He began to study those other young men on the Underground, trying to separate the wolves from the ewes. He found it next to impossible to distinguish a sharpened umbrella point from a satisfied middle class stick-in-the-mud.

And, for a final try-out, he visited Mrs. Bernice Hale one evening by appointment. The killing he'd made from the queer's suite could be dented, but never fully given away.

"I've saved some money," Joe said as he reached ten quid across to her. "I promised to repay..."

"Oh, Joe!" Tears moistened the woman's eyes. She took the cash and hurriedly wrote a receipt. "I..." She wiped her eyes with a cheap cotton handkerchief. "My son would like to know you, Joe." She reached the slip across to her protégé. "It isn't often our judgement is justified, but you're the exception to the rule. It makes all our efforts worthwhile."

Joe felt like a louse until he gave due consideration to his own ambitions. It had been more than a good gesture making one simple repayment of his outstanding loans. It had got him in solid. Now; anything, any time... "Are you sure you can afford this?"

"I'm sure."

"You must be living on a meagre budget."

"I'm existing."

"Well, Joe, if you should ever..." She hesitated. A brief flash in his eyes disturbed her.

"I think I'll be able to manage alone, Mrs. Hale."

Thrusting doubt into dark, forgetting recesses, she smiled. "Keep in touch, Joe. I'd like to know what you are doing and be able to quote you as an example for other unfortunates to follow."

Getting to the door, Joe dropped the hint he thought would bring her running. "You've got my address, Mrs. Hale. If you ever want to visit me I'll be home. I haven't found that girl yet..." He waved nonchalantly and made a hasty exit. But not before he caught a brief glimpse of her face. It gave him hope. He liked to imagine she was lonely – doing without. If only...

*

Soho at night was no place for a City type. Certainly not an affluent young man alone. Joe didn't give a damn. He could handle himself better than most of the long-haired touts flogging their wares. Almost as well as the heavy boys menacing frightened tourists into taking a walk down a back alley to watch a series of blue films performed by the most brazen of brass and defeated layabouts. Joe knew all the tricks or thought he did. After all, he had worked for "God" recently...

Lethargic crowds paraded the maze, seeking pleasures for a price. Hurrying inhabitants of the rabbit warren hawked their bulky packages of pornographic books in sight of strolling fuzz. Brass kept alert eyes peeled from bedroom windows as pimps worked their charms on possible targets in a variety of sleazy clubs and near-beer joints. The young didn't require pimping services. They got it free, for kicks, or for a pill or two. They got it better than the nervous, introvertish lecher afraid to ask for "special treatment". The youth cult had taken over old Soho. The coffee bars, the invasion of freelancing teenage nymphs and the vicious gangs roaming what had always been a stable belonging to older, wiser, shadowy figures had changed the area. Old-timers could no longer compete. Youth demanded, and refused to run scared of Manson "gods". Drugs gave courage and ill-advised bravado.

Joe considered the scene with a discriminating gaze. He was not interested in the flighty bits displaying their thighs nor the coaxing pleas of his generation trying to ensnare what they believed to be a provincial mark into a dark, over-priced den where even the ginger beer was watered.

Joe wanted companionship. Not womanship. He wanted to find his own... Dean Street, Frith Street, Old Compton Street, Greek Street. He walked them all; leisurely, alert. He saw the sweating bald-headed ones dart from dirty bookshops with a wrapped parcel clutched feverishly in clammy hands. Saw tarted-up birds from Ilford, Battersea, Highbury and a score of other outlying districts scamper between clubs. They were easy to spot. Heavy eye shadow, hungry lean features, shimmering sweaters hoisting up fake breasts. Small make-up cases swinging to the beat of their tight, not-fleshed-enough bottoms. He saw the rolling drunks, the pop-eyed trippers, the swaggering thugs showing off a new horse-blanket made into a suit.

And there were the prowling cars with their look-everywhere-save-the-road drivers creeping from skirt to skirt hopefully affecting a it's-the-traffic-congestion-that-makes-me-drive-slow attitude.

There were cops and detectives. There were ordinary decent tourists or Londoners out for an exotic meal in one of the dozen or so famous restaurants. There were hard-working bartenders and waitresses going and coming as shifts started and ended. There were wide-boys studying passing faces for a good old-fashioned "steamer". There was Danny, Freddie, Bob, Fat John, Robin, Kenny, Harry, Angie, Mary, Molly and – always – Julie. Flies stuck in the ointment called Soho. Dying flies all. Too steeped in the terrible rat race, the daily routine to seek greener fields.

To think he had once considered this the acme of ambition! He wanted to belong to the West End – not Soho's grubby counterfeit acres. He wanted to be acceptable in that luxurious quarter adjoining this barbaric haven – the one across Regent Street. The one called Mayfair. That's where the money was – in every sense.

But he was inside Soho's hellhole. Looking for one sign. Searching for another who felt exactly as he did.

He had about given up hope when he entered Shaftesbury Avenue a third time. Traffic moved faster here. The people did not have those hard-bitten eyes now. These were theatre-goers and Soho-proper avoidees.

The youth came out of the coffee bar and stood momentarily alone on the pavement. Joe tensed.

A gaggle of chattering females descended on the youth and he quickly moved. Joe followed through fume-spluming taxis down into Rupert Street. Do-nothing teenagers hung around doorways leading upstairs to juke-box squalor. Music blasted into the drawing night like great blankets of sound enshrouding those not in sympathy with modern noise.

A queer minced into sight, blond(e) locks flying in a slight breeze, perfume wafting from his floral shirt in waves. *If he wasn't in such an exposed position I'd kick his sexy-ass*, Joe thought delightedly. Queer-bashing was not on the cards tonight, though. Some other time he could vent his hatred and capitalise from the pleasure.

The youth paused as he reached Leicester Square. Joe could feel his indecision – right, or left. To the Tube or back into Piccadilly Circus. Home or mixing with the drug-pushers forming their nightly queue as the desperate ones drifted into town.

Joe reached the youth's side. "I'm Joe Hawkins... mind if I join you?" He sounded too polite. That's what working under Totter's gimlet gaze did for him!

The youth stepped back a pace and deliberately studied Joe's mode of dress. "Do you read...?" he started to ask with carefully modulated tones.

"Articles mentioning how suedeheads should dress?"

The youth smiled broadly. He nodded and tipped his bowler with an exaggerated welcoming gesture.

"You, too?" Joe asked tightly.

"Me, also!" came the easy reply. "I say, this is rather nice."

Joe shuddered inside where his East End skinhead longings still manifested some aversion to plum-in-the-mouthisms. He forced himself to remember his ambitions to rise above the common herd. He would have to accept an Oxford accent as he would have to refrain from instantaneous explosion whenever he heard those hoity-toity assumed sayings of the Mayfair fraternity. He was not to know then that the characteristics were as false as the strippers' bursting tits.

"We're a rare breed," the youth said over traffic roar. "Not many of us about, eh what?"

"I was beginning to wonder if I was the only one," Joe laughed.

"Not quite, old chap. There are others. I guarantee that."

Controlling an urge to turn tail and run for cover Joe asked: "How did you decide to join *us*?"

The youth flicked a speck of imaginary dust from his expensive Crombie coat. "What does that mean?" he asked suspiciously.

"I was a skinhead," Joe replied honestly.

"Oh!" There was a slight tinge of disappointment in the voice. "A skinhead!" That sounded like a curse.

"What were you?"

For a few seconds the youth stood frozen in deep dark thought. Then, suddenly, he relaxed. He was as tall as Joe, handsome without being attractive, and sported a huge solitaire diamond ring which flashed in the headlight passing of cars.

Joe shuffled his feet as the suspense mounted. What the hell was wrong with this guy? Couldn't he give a straight answer? Or was he pretending to be a suedehead and mocking me? In another second Joe's fists would have dented that smile.

"Mate..."and the vocal inflection changed drastically, "I'm like you – an ex-skinhead. Chelsea Shed type."

Joe laughed softly, letting the tension within him then vaporise in a loud guffaw. "I thought you were from..."

"Some expensive college?"

"Yeah!"

"Shit on them! I was born in Shepherd's Bush."

"Up Plaistow and The Hammers!"

"A year ago I'd have done you for that!"

"A year ago me mates would have backed The Hammers."

"I've been inside," the youth said quietly next.

Joe hesitated. Confessions like this came hard after all those efforts to cover tracks.

"You've done bird, too!" the youth accused.

"The Scrubs," Joe admitted with reluctance.

"Derby, me." Their "old school tie bit" broadened conversation. "I met some big men there."

"I ignored 'em all," Joe said as if he had been the biggest man in The Scrubs.

"How did they nick you?"

Joe stood straight, proud still. "I done a sergeant in Hyde Park."

"I beat up on a Pakki and stole his savings."

"They gave you bird for that?" Joe sounded and felt amazed at such injustice.

"He was hospitalised for sixteen weeks," the youth explained. "And I got away with five thousand."

"They took it back," Joe said knowingly.

"Like hell they did! I hid it all."

Joe wanted to scream. The next question was so very important. "What did the magistrate give you for that?"

The youth's gloating rose above traffic, passers-by, London's beating heart. Beating his mental breast for the world to witness his harsh sentence, he moaned: "I got a lousy eighteen months for doing a fuzz!"

"We all learn by our mistakes," the youth said, pouring on the misery.

"Have you got the cash?"

"Most every penny."

"And what next?"

The youth bent forward and whispered directly into Joe's receptive ear: "I'm going to make it work for me. I've got a plan..."

Joe didn't give a damn what plans the Shed bastard had. He had a few of his own. If only he could get his hands on that amount of money! God, what a haul! What a lovely set-up he'd landed himself in!

"I've a friend," the youth explained secretly. "He's got connections and I've promised to invest in his operation. I stand to double my loot in forty eight hours if all goes well."

"And if it doesn't?" Joe wanted to know.

"Shit, we all make mistakes as the telly commercial says."

That was poor policy according to Joe's current thoughts. A guy with five thousand in the sock should have more than a fifty-fifty chance. He should *command* a definite seven grand profit. No less. In this era money talked. More than in bygones. Especially illicit reserves. They spoke hardest, highest. What with inflation round the corner, bank loans tough to get and a semi-squeeze on, the guy with loot in hand had to be kingpin of all he surveyed.

"Have you handed him the money yet?" Joe asked.

The youth narrowed his eyes and pierced Joe with a menacing stare. "You're wanting an awful lot of information, mate. What if I have or haven't? Is it any concern of yours?"

Joe smiled to allay the other's naturally suspicious nature. "I don't give a damn. I was just being friendly."

"With friends who stick unwanted noses in who needs enemies!" came the retort.

"Okay... okay, forget I mentioned it."

"Forgotten, mate!" the youth held out his hand and they shook. "I'm Terry Walker. How about a drink?"

"Over there?" Joe nodded at the Green Dragon.

"No, thanks. There are too many ears in places like that. I know a small intimate club not far away. Care to become a member?"

"Not if it costs me."

"It won't. I guarantee that." The noise of a skidding car blocked his next sentence and when the taxi driver involved in a near miss got tired of the sound of his own voice Joe asked: "What was that you said?"

Terry grinned and tilted his bowler to a carefree angle. "I said we might find a couple of dollybirds, too."

"Nothing doing if they're Soho tarts."

"This club is in Mayfair, mate. Only the best for us suedeheads, eh?" He began walking down Shaftesbury Avenue with Joe matching stride for stride. The youth walked fast and Joe was out of puff when they finally entered a narrow, twisting street partway up Regent Street. Opening a door, Terry paused at the bottom of steep stairs. "No name. No publicity. Members only and no cops allowed."

When Terry pushed him through a padded door which effectively deadened the sound coming from a L-shaped bar, Joe was instantly conscious of alert eyes watching his every move. There were about fifteen people in the bar – all with that quiet reserve associated with a better class Englishman. A brunette barmaid leant her small breasts on the counter and said: "Sorry – we only..." Her face broke into a large smile as Terry came into view. "Oh, you're with a member. That's fine. Come on, take a pew."

Joe let Terry settle his rump on a stool first and took stock of the barmaid. She was in her middle thirties, vivacious, darker skinned than the usual London girl, and she wore a mini-skirt which permitted the customers to see her very shapely thighs right to the flare of her buttocks.

"How about a membership card for my friend, Joe Hawkins?" Terry asked disinterestedly. His attention was focused on a slot machine standing idle in an end of the "L".

"Tokens, Terry?"

"A couple of quids' worth, Vera. I feel lucky tonight."

"Monica got the jackpot last Wednesday. I don't know if it's worth chasing."

"How much?" Terry asked.

"Sixteen pounds exactly."

"About ten of that belonged to me." The youth grinned, tossing his hat at a carved eagle. Apparently he made a habit of this feat. The bowler shook and firmly rested on the eagle's beak.

.Vera slid a card across her counter in Joe's direction. "What'll it be gents?"

"Something strong and sexy," Terry chided.

"Pink gin?"

"Hell, no. Rum and Coke."

"And you, sir?" Joe loved the "sir". Having to call old Trotter and the senior partners "sir" every day of his working week had made him yearn to get the same treatment elsewhere. "I'll have a large Scotch with soda."

"How about this?" Terry asked softly as Vera attended to their drinks. "Each of those blokes is worth a hundred thousand and more."

Joe glanced down the bar. The men in question stood in a small group engaged in almost whispered discussion. It was evident they were dealing with business queries from the number of times they referred to catalogues and printed broadsheets.

"Who are they?" Joe asked.

"Antique dealers. They're part of a ring."

Joe had heard about such things although he did not know how rings operated nor why they were supposed to be illegal. He did understand the amount of money to be made from antiques though. Providing one had knowledge, that was.

"What about them?" He gestured at another group.

Terry shrugged casually. "Society layabouts. They've got money but more credit than a bank account. I wouldn't waste time on them."

"Is your friend here?"

Terry placed a hand across Joe's blank application card. "We were going to forget that."

"Sorry." Deliberately now, Joe removed the youth's hand and asked: "Got a pen?"

"Before you fill it in – where do you live?"

"A flatlet in Bayswater."

"Not good enough. Use my address..." A pen and business card were placed next to the application. "It's phoney but it gets results. Make it 'care of' the office..."

Joe was discovering there was a lot to this Mayfair con-game. The card Terry used said he was a director of William Blakison & Partners, Property Management Consultants. The address was in the City and there was also a telephone number. "Is this real?" Joe asked, pointing at the number.

"Sure it is. That's where I work. I have a cubby-hole of an office with a private line."

"Your own office?"

"Use your noggin' mate. No! I'm not a director or anything like that. I'm a glorified message boy."

"Why work when you've got loot?" Joe was confused.

"'Cause the bloody cops are still trying to find my cash, stupid." Vera came with the drinks and Terry's tokens. Taking his rum and the one-armed bandit's fodder the youth hurried to the machine.

"He certainly has gambling fever," Vera said confidentially.

"Yes," Joe murmured and began writing. He didn't enjoy being left alone with the woman. If she questioned him too closely he might give Terry's game away. When he completed the application he pushed it back at Vera and quickly went to Terry's side.

"I thought you'd be raping Vera by now," the youth remarked.

"Is she...?"

"Easy. We've all had her."

"I'm only here for the beer," Joe laughed to cover his inability to mingle freely with these people. If it had been the East End he could have handled any situation but there was a barrier somewhere inside him when it boiled down to leaping into the high income gathering. His was a fumbling in the darkest night effort to get to grips with a new way of life. The mistakes he would surely make could not be allowed to happen in this his first Mayfair jaunt. Later, once he solo-ed he would brush aside those little embarrassments and treat them as experience gained. Not tonight. Not alone. Vera could wait. The day would dawn soon enough for her brand of passion.

"Take your bloody hat off. Hang your umbrella on a hook. Relax. Nobody's going to debag you, Joe." Another token slid into the machine and the wheels whirred as Terry manipulated the lever to some secret pattern of pressure.

Coming back to Terry with his drink in one hand and a cigarette in the other, Joe asked: "How did you learn to talk their language?"

"I studied books. Novels about dollybirds and Mayfair rogues. I went into Bond Street shops and listened. It didn't take long to twig what they said and how they said it."

Joe admired the Chelsea skinhead's... ex-skinhead's... determination to break loose and establish his name in society. Frankly, Joe didn't read much. Headlines in the *Standard* or the sports news in the *Mirror*. A few times every year he bought a racy, sexy paperback but he seldom finished those. Once he devoured the violence and the sex he flung it away.

Three oranges came up for Terry and he scooped the coins into his hand. "Best way to get with it, Joe is to take one of their women to bed." Another token vanished into the machine's greedy jaw. "These birds talk all the while. They don't ever stop chatting about what is happening."

"Do you ever get into punch-ups?"

Terry scowled. "Not unless I have to."

"Don't you miss an aggro?"

"Bloody right, mate..." Terry glanced around. "Drop it, Joe."

"You going to play that thing all night?" The infernal whirr, clatter, tink of the machine was driving Joe nuts. He felt tight inside. The sensation was an old one. Back in the old days when his mates were with him he'd have found some bastard to kick or some bovver to relieve his tensions. Now, what was there to do? Bloody nothing! If it hadn't been for Terry's loot and a slim chance of getting his fingers on some of it he'd have taken off right then. Instead, he stayed – and suffered, and bought fresh drinks contrary to the rules of strictly membership clubs...

CHAPTER SEVEN

FOUR OILY sardines stared up at him from the dark toast. An open tin containing a few broken bodies lay beside his teacup like a cramped communal graveyard recently violated. "What a bloody breakfast!" he swore at the Norwegian product. He'd been skimping on food lately. Getting a wardrobe of suitable clothes counted for more than filling his stomach with the kind of food would-be Mayfair clan considered barely adequate to sustain flesh.

He thumped a ketchup bottle, spilling sauce on sardines and naked thighs. Fingering the spilt ketchup back on to his plate he gazed across the small table to where a breeze blew his curtains aside from an open window. Directly across the street he could see the old biddy peeping from the shadowy interior of her room. He didn't give a damn if she got a kick out of watching his total nudity. He enjoyed eating breakfast in the buff. He felt like flashing it at her but decided to concentrate on the bloody sardines instead.

Attacking the insipid meal he thought about last night. That Terry was a cagey bastard. All he knew for sure was that the deal would be made today at Baker Street underground station. Nothing else. He was invited to be present for what he conjectured would be a highly crooked transaction. There was no inkling how many others would attend the great ceremony nor if he would ever get the slightest opportunity to grab off a few hundred for himself.

That was the horrible dilemma for Joe. He wanted in with Terry but he wanted to make a profit from their association. And he knew that any sleight of hand on his part would alienate the new friendship. He liked being a member of a posh club but if he double-crossed the youth he could not return there. Not unless he wanted to risk getting the hell kicked out of his hide. An ex-skinhead could revert to bovver boots if the occasion was provocative enough.

Spearing a defenceless sardine from its tin he told it: "I'd be worse off than you poor bastards. I'd be crippled – you're dead already!"

If only he could get his old mob back in action. They'd bleedin' take care of Terry's mates.

"Christ! Cut it out!"

The words exploded in the room, his head. Seizing the dirty dishes he dropped them into the sink and stared at his reflection in a stained mirror over it.

"The blokes you're meeting don't say bleedin'," he told the unshaved image. "They don't wish for mates, they don't give a damn about anything. Think posh, talk posh, act posh – and bloody do the screw-happy lot of 'em when you can."

He grinned and scratched his shoulder blade. Walking to the window he stood in full naked view of the woman over there. He made a gesture she could not fail to understand and saw a shape flit back into the dark interior away from the curtains. If only she would leave those curtains apart sometime he might get a peep and see if she was a worthwhile target for his frustrations.

Turning from the window, he considered what to wear. He wanted a change from the City suit and bowler. It may be a symbol of what he had become – in part. But a change did a guy good. He'd spent his ill-gotten gains extravagantly. He still had a nest-egg but he was nursing that. This room was getting on his wick. He wanted a bigger, better pad. One with private bath and decent kitchen, separate bedroom and a fashionable lounge. He'd studied these things recently; listened to the office wallahs talking about their mews cottage, or the flat in St.

John's Wood, or the pater's town house. Dissatis-faction burned at his guts like hell's fires. Going up in the world meant an abode to match one's opin-ion of oneself.

Carefully selecting a frilled shirt, he put that on then flung it aside when he felt his stubbled chin. Quickly, he washed, shaved, applied talc and deo-dorant. He didn't favour the smells but his in-crowd insisted they were vital. Now, he donned the shirt, and buttoned it. Next, he chose a dark blue suit and highly polished shoes to match; a floral wide tie, brilliant white socks and lightweight cream-colour-ed gloves. He would not wear a hat but his umbrel-la belonged. It was, for Joe, a suedehead's "bovver boots" insignia. Anyway, if Terry got nasty the um-brella was his weapon of escape. He fondled the sharp tip. He'd done a marvellous job on it – just like a sword point and skilfully blackened so not to attract undue attention from the uptight mob.

He frowned. Perhaps he should apply a covering coat of brass-gold paint to make it appear more like an authentic metal tip. He wished he could afford to buy a sword-stick – always providing he could find a dealer stupid enough to flog him one. That was the trouble with items classified as dangerous by the police. Dealers seldom left themselves open to... *Hey, wait a mo!* he thought. Those blokes in Terry's club were antique merchants. If he could get the goods on one of 'em he might make a blackmailing switch. Sword-stick for dropping out of the picture.

"They're worse than any heavy mob," he told himself after a few minutes exciting contemplation. "They'd cut me into so many bloody pieces I'd be lucky to have a leg left for burial."

It had been a lovely thought though. One to forget in the light of cold, hard reasoning. He didn't want undue trouble. Terry was bovver enough for the moment.

*

Drugs – that's what they're bargaining for!

Joe stood frozen as the realisation struck home. Terry didn't need to tell him anything. He recognised those samples being secretively passed from hand to hand – all except his, naturally. He was the outsider looking in; the guy who wasn't there.

"A quick sale'll make you two cool grand, mate," a thick-necked man was saying to Terry. He got his samples back and dropped them into a jacket pocket. "I'll give you a few addresses for starters."

"How come *you* don't flog the stuff?" Terry asked with suspicion shadowing his features.

"You must be jokin'," the man snorted. "The fuzz know me by sight. I'd get within a mile of Soho and the bastards would nick the lot."

"Has it got to be right in Soho?"

Joe had the same idea. Something about the deal stank. He couldn't see a middle man backing off from a handsome profit this close to payday.

The man shuffled, passing a handkerchief across a sweat-filmed forehead. "Sonny, lemme explain how we operate. I import it, have it mixed and packaged and up the ante to include my rake-off. You take the big – and I mean BIG – risk getting in touch with the street pushers. I'm not a mug. I want a return on my investment – not two, maybe three years."

"I still can't see why you..." Terry mumbled.

"Crissakes, it's bleedin' simple," the man said in exasperation. "I'm not goin' to push the stuff. I'm selling for a big price. You make yours and we all go home happy. Okay?"

Terry turned to his mate – a small, fat guy with glasses and pimples on his neck. He dressed neat but no amount of new clothes would ever make him appear more than a cheap spiv.

"How about it, Fred?"

"It's up to you, Terry. I like the deal."

Terry's eyes flashed at Joe. "And you?" he asked.

Joe hesitated. There were a few questions he would have liked to ask but just putting himself that far into the picture would have given away his ultimate aims. "Do we have to cart loads of packages in plain sight of the law?"

The man chuckled. "Easy seen you kids are rank amateurs," he said sarcastically. "It's all in those lockers..." He pointed at a row of storage lockers nearby and produced six keys from a trouser pocket. "Each locker has enough stuff to make one delivery. There are three of you. If the fuzz gets wise then you don't lose too much profit."

"Hey," Joe said. "If they grab the stuff they also grab the bloke."

"S'truth..." Terry exclaimed.

"Jeeze," the man exhaled. "Don't tell me you haven't thought about getting nicked?"

Terry covered fast. "Of course we have, old chap."

The man laughed. "Old chap? God, you kids!"

"I'll take it," Terry said suddenly. "Pay the man, Fred."

As Fred handed over Terry's cash, the youth drew Joe aside. "Are you in with us?" he asked.

Joe hesitated dramatically. He was in – right up to getting a few of those locker keys. But he wanted Terry to believe he felt apprehensive. It wouldn't do to jump too fast. Not now. Not knowing how bloody suspicious his new mate could be. "Well..."

"Ahhh, come on, Joe. I need your help. I'll pay."

"How much?"

"Half of what we make on your deliveries. How's that?"

"Fair," Joe allowed. "I'm in, Terry."

The youth breathed relief. "God, this is not going to be a quick turn-over," he said softly. "We've got to find buyers."

"Your friend mentioned some addresses," Joe reminded.

Terry tore back to Fred. Speaking to the man he asked: "Where's the addresses?"

The man wadded the money into his small case which had been ready by his left leg all through the discussion. "Got a pencil and paper?"

Terry found an old envelope and used Fred's pen. The man reeled off five names and club addresses adding a few words of caution after each. One struck Joe as being a complete waste of time when the man said: "He always takes deliveries in the club as he makes his contacts. You may wait a few hours but he's not mean. You'll get top whack there."

Like being a sitting duck for any cop doing an undercover job, Joe thought. *That one is not for me!*

An idea lit up Joe's brain. A brilliant notion for getting away with his haul and not having Terry on his back. One of those million-to-a-quid brainwaves. He felt immensely better for having had the solution to his problem landed right inside his mind.

At last, the locker keys changed hands and the man lost himself in the growing crowds fighting their way in and out of the station. Joe noticed another man join their late associate, and smiled.

Trust that type to bring along protection in case the buyers decided to pull a fast one!

Terry rubbed his hands and chuckled. "We've got it made, mates," he announced. "Let's get started..."

*

By seven-thirty exactly, Joe had collected six hundred quid near enough. He had given Terry the bulk of it and kept his profit percentage – a mere eighty five pounds. Fred had departed for his third contact's pad and Terry was all set to send Joe into the lion's den when Joe suddenly said: "I got a tip from my last sucker."

Terry's face tensed. "Bad news?"

Joe laughed and slapped the youth on the back. "Great news, mate!" He eased two packets into his pocket, hating the way they spoilt the cut of his jacket. "I'll have an extra lot. This guy gave me a sure thing. Said he'd personally make a telephone call and describe me in advance."

Terry frowned at the envelope in his hand – the one with the address of their last contact. "I wanted you to handle this, Joe," he said slowly. "I could make your delivery and explain..."

"Too late for that, Terry," Joe said apologetically. "I can't get hold of this bloke again and he did say how..."

"Hell!" Terry exploded. "Okay, it's all loot. When you've got the money meet me here. Looks like I'll be there for a few hours."

Joe studied the address carefully and nodded. "Is Fred coming along too?"

"Yeah. We might as well finish the day having a few drinks. We can unload the last lockers tomorrow night."

"I won't be long, Terry. Let me have those five packages, eh? If my man doesn't take 'em I can bring it back to your bloke." Joe held his breath. This was the vital moment.

Without anticipating trouble, Terry handed the extra over. *Probably trusts me after all*, Joe thought. *A typical Shed idiot!*

Waving his farewell, Joe sauntered into the mainstream of traffic, moving down into the bowels of London's rabbit warren. When he reached the bottom he waited five minutes and hurried back to the lockers. One was empty and he emptied his pockets, placed a coin in the slot and removed the key. Whistling and twirling his umbrella, he walked out into Baker Street and across the road to a pub. Two large Hundred Pipers' and he went back to the underground station. There were telephones inside and his call was most important...

CHAPTER EIGHT

THE STORY had been buried inside the newspaper. Joe read it with unsuppressed excitement as his train slowed at Marble Arch. He had expected a front page banner headline, but he appreciated the eventual outcome of his tip-off regardless.

LONDON DRUG RAID...

Police last night raided the premises of Soho's Oblique Club and confiscated a large quantity of narcotics. Two men are presently facing charges following an anonymous telephone call. The club management denied any connection with the men. A spokesman told our reporter: "We operate within the law. Any member suspected of using drugs is automatically out."

The Oblique Club is normally frequented by teenagers and has a good reputation although, as the owners point out, "Rotten apples are found in every barrel and I suppose we're no exception."

The men are due to appear this morning at magistrate's court.

The locker key felt very comfortable in Joe's pocket. He could afford to allow a few days to pass before capitalising on Terry's *misfortune.*

Smiling at a bird seated across the aisle, Joe calmly progressed to the sports pages. Nothing old Totter would say today could damp his high spirits. Tonight he had a date with Lois. In this mood she would lose her cherished – but hardly priceless – possession. He would buy a bottle and ask her to help him find a decent flat somewhere closer to Mayfair. Being a suedehead had more compensations than being crowned king of all skinheads. What did he need with gangs backing him! He had accomplished a masterful stroke without even resorting to violence. Not that he would ever outgrow the basic need to use force whenever the occasion demanded, or whenever he felt it necessary to relieve pent-up frustrations. The world was a savage place and only the strong and the brutal could ever rightfully claim a niche. That was his thinking!

Letting the paper slip on to his lap, Joe tried to calculate how much he was currently worth. He had his "commission money" kindly paid by Terry for "services about to be rendered". That was a bloody good laugh! Getting paid to double-cross a mate! The fool! He had a locker key and inside that locker a cool four hundred quid's worth of pot. At market prices, that was. He'd find a buyer, make the deal and drop out from the scene. He didn't like messing around with drugs. The profits were fantastic but he had an aversion. Nothing to do with morality. Just – it wasn't his pitch.

Almost five hundred sounded nice in his mind. With that kind of loot he could easily afford to splash out on decent food, more top notch gear, a snazzy flat and a couple of birds. Not just Lois, although making her was of paramount importance. He did not like admitting failure. She would be his. Tonight. After her, there would be others. Ones used to performing bloody wonders and not bothered about getting pregnant or betraying daddy's trust. God, that was a lark. Imagine a bird in this day and age keeping herself whole because she had promised daddy! It was unbelievable. Fantastically so.

The newspaper dropped to the floor and went unnoticed by Joe. He was way ahead of the present – this dreary day with its breathless waiting for events to mature. Everything he had read about suedeheads made him want to develop his talents to the exquisite point offering ambition's fulfilment.

If he had to appear above suspicion he would, of necessity be compelled to belong to some notable, worthy youth fraternity. That meant questions in the office. Some of his snooty-nosed workmates attended clubs specifically aimed at helping out less fortunates than themselves. Joe would get some names and make enquiries. When he found the one he reckoned would suit his purposes best he would join. Until then, he had more than sufficient to be getting along with... Lois, flogging the dope, finding new accommodation...

Lois's large, luminous blue eyes widened in surprise when she saw the liquor bottles arrayed on a table. She did not know that Joe had bought the reproduction sofa table on his way home especially for the occasion... well, not quite especially. He would need decent furniture when he got his close-to-Mayfair flat. This was a start and making an impression at the same time. He had also splurged on drink – a bottle of Hundred Pipers, Captain Morgan Rum, Noilly Prat and several types of mix.

"Joe, how much do you think you can drink?" she asked with a pleasant smile.

He placed his bowler on a peg and removed his coat and jacket. "Get comfortable, Lois and forget about putting a limit on booze. Let me have your sweater."

"That's all you're getting, Joe," she replied firmly as he helped remove the pearl-studded Austrian sweater. He could tell it was expensive from the way it felt.

Ignoring her remark which was too pointed to please, he poured a treble Scotch into each glass and added the minimum mix. Even with the window open the flatlet was hot – clammy hot. And he could see the old biddy across the street doing her peeping from behind those static curtains. God, he hoped she'd get an eyeful tonight! If she was that bloody frustrated she'd have an emotional kitten when he began stripping Lois.

Handing the glass to Lois he said: "Cheers," and settled on the bed. "I'd like to ask a favour of you, Lois," he said finally as she prowled the room sipping her drink and pulling faces at its strength. "I'm not happy living here and I thought you'd like to help me find another place – nearer the West End; something better."

Her shoulders moved in a shrug which only served to emphasise her lovely breasts. She was wearing a frilly blouse, a – of all things – suede skirt down to mid-thigh, tights and flat-heeled shoes. Her hair was still tied in a knot at the nape of her slender neck – ready, Joe believed, to be untied and caressed as passions began to rise.

"Why me?"

"You've got taste. You're extra special in my estimation." He hid a grin. Terry had suggested reading books and he had. One. The line came directly from that! Admittedly the book lay under his bed open at page twenty three. He was a painfully slow reader but his memory for things which could progress his ambitions was excellent.

Lois preened self-consciously. She adored men paying her unsolicited compliments. Joe grew a foot in stature in *her* estimation! "Thanks for that, Joe. I'd be glad to assist you."

He had his campaign all mapped out. First the feint, then the lull to throw the enemy off balance until, finally, the main body was sent in to totally destroy opposition.

"I'm so tired," he lied. "My back aches something awful."

Lois came and sat on the bed beside him.

"Would you like to massage me?" he asked softly.

"I'm not much good at that."

"Every little counts."

She sipped her randy-making drink again, face slightly flushed already. "Where?" she asked politely.

He grinned, began removing his shirt. Her eyes blinked, staring unkindly. He quickly explained: "You can't massage weary muscles through a shirt."

She accepted his excuse and waited until he lay along the bed. He was muscular, with no unsightly fat on his young body. Her hands went unerringly to his shoulders and began to knead the flesh. He groaned in simulated ecstasy.

"Lovely, Lois. I could have this done to me all night."

"Not by me!" Her hands temporarily ceased their ministrations.

He sat upright and finished his drink. Gesturing for her to follow suit he poured fresh supplies – making the second one stronger still. Seated beside her he raised his glass, drank half in one go. He had, apparently, never heard of moderation. "Want to massage me again?"

She felt slightly woozy. "Only for a minute," she said.

Flat on his stomach with her tender hands sliding over his skin Joe sensed the moment right for that lull. He moaned. "Thanks, Lois. You're sweet..." *Another line from the book.* He twisted around to face her. "Have you ever had a massage?"

She sampled her drink. "Once. After a Turkish bath."

"Did you like it?"

"Smashing!" She giggled. "I'm getting sloshed, Joe."

"On two drinks?" he asked.

"They're strong."

"Don't you drink much?" He knew she didn't.

"Not much," she confessed. "And I haven't eaten yet."

"We'll go out for dinner, eh?"

She nodded. "I think we should – and soon."

He avoided saying when they would eat. "A friend of mine taught me how to massage," he said nonchalantly. *The campaign was reaching a crucial stage.*

"Oh!" her eyes suggested interest.

"Would you like me to show you?"

"Do I have to take my blouse off?"

"But not your brassiere," he joked.

That seemed to satisfy her sense of decency. Without a word she removed the blouse to reveal breasts barely concealed in a half-cup bra. It was all he could do to refrain from taking those beautiful orbs from their exciting cups and showering them with lustful kisses.

"On your tummy," he commanded.

When his fingers began to knead her silken flesh he deliberately hooked himself into her brassiere straps several times before saying: "I can't get the right sweep to this with that on."

She rose on an elbow, took another drink. "Joe..."

"I promise no tricks, Lois," he said hurriedly.

"Oh, hell!" Her hands came back and unhooked the offending straps. She held the front cups tight against her breasts and sank back on the bed.

Slowly, he massaged her spine... up, down, around. Like a spider spinning a web he covered her entire back, moving in the direction of her sides, on to the lovely surface of those exciting breasts, under her armpits.

"Like it?"

She moaned. "Lovely."

"If I could get to the base of your spine..." Without thinking she writhed, unzipped her suede skirt and pushed that and her tights down to reveal the thrilling curves of her gorgeous buttocks. The top of her brief panties showed and in seconds his fingers worked them down... down... until all her bottom was uncovered.

The final attack was due!

His fingers curled round her exquisite curves... probing regions not normally included in the masseurs' attentions. Her gentle undulations encouraged him; her gasping sent him into a tizzy of uncontrolled brashness.

"Lois..." he panted turning her onto her back, hands now demanding as they pushed the offending clothing down... to reveal in entirety.

Her chestnut hair had loosened and spread to frame her face. Her eyes closed, her mouth pleading for his hot kisses.

Watch this! Joe mentally told the old biddy across the street. He tore his clothes from him, flung himself down on the bed with Lois surrendering to his adventurous gropings. His tongue darted into her open mouth, his fingers curled into her tights and panties as her legs came up to facilitate the completion of her abandonment.

In those precious seconds before he mounted her, Joe thought: *She's better than anything I've ever had...* and then her flesh held him in a vice, her desire a seething, boiling mass which could not be denied...

CHAPTER NINE

LIKE A KING in residence in his castle Joe marched from room to room and luxuriated in the knowledge that his deflowering of Lois had not been without its compensations. She had been terrific. He understood now why some men *insisted* on having a virgin to bed when the experienced world of professional women was always available. But there was more to Lois than mere sex although that had been quite a thrilling lesson in the "unknown".

Lois had society tastes which he could not begin to understand. She had helped him select the average flat for an up-and-coming young executive without knowing that his income was strictly derived from illicit activities. The amount his office paid would furnish a bedsitter in Balham, nothing more.

It had been four weeks since he last bedded Lois. After the initial ritual she had grown less attractive, less interesting. Her notions of security, marriage and children scared the hell out of him. Anyway, he never had any intentions of sticking with her. Her virginity had been the prime target. Once that went, so did his desire to count her amongst his "friends".

He frowned at an Empire mirror with twin candlestick sconces. What friends did he have? Since going "inside" he had been alone. There had been Terry and, of course, Lois. But they had not been friends. They were people to be used. Mrs. Hale tried to befriend him, but unless she could offer something sexual she would remain a means to an unending source of quick loans.

He was friendless!

He was nature's castigated soul!

Laughing as he strolled from master bedroom to lounge he again marvelled at the compactness, the luxuriousness of this elite flat. Sixteen guineas per week for what should have cost twice as much. Lois had been invaluable. *An associate of daddy's had informed her of a place he wished to rent.* Naturally, as a close social acquaintance he would let it go for less than market value! Naturally! Half-price yet!

God, what bleedin fools these upper-class people were! How the hell did they ever make the money they had when the old school tie governed their every move?

On the open market the flat would easily have fetched £40 per week inclusive. Joe knew. He had studied the ads in the *Evening Standard*. Places less than a street away went for sixty per week. Exclusive, too. And this one was tastefully and completely furnished.

Lois had demonstrated her "in" with snobland. No references. No guarantees. Just a simple lease and a fifty quid deposit against undue wear-and-tear on the furnishings. One week's rent in advance and – hey, presto – he had arrive in style! What a place compared to his Plaistow home!

In every way he ruled supreme. Authentic antiques as against Co-op furnishings of the cheapest variety. Spacious rooms and wall-to-wall carpets when he had been used to cramped surroundings and threadbare rugs trying to cover ugly floorboards. A modern American-style kitchen with all the latest gimmicks. His mother still cooked on an ancient gas stove and used utensils so thin on the bottom they could almost be used as sieves.

He went to the front windows – plural. From one he could see Marble Arch. From the other an expanse of expensive flats above elite shops. The windows had lace curtains and heavy velvet drapes to match the decor of the lounge. The fireplace was large and suitable for burning yule logs fifty-two weeks in the year. There was even an extractor fan in the room and fan heaters which blew cool air in summer or hot in winter if lighting a fire proved too much of a chore.

According to the owner, the porter collected the garbage every second day and a maid was available if one wished to shell out an additional £1.50 per week. Joe didn't bother with the service. He had a vacuum cleaner and could do that much for himself. Or would until Dame Fortune smiled more benevolently on him! His money would not last forever. With the coppers hot in Soho he had been lucky getting a quick one-shot sale for the drugs at a rock bottom price, bringing him £375. And stupid bastards like Terry did not grow on trees. Not in Brooklyn or in London!

He grinned at the leather-bound bookshelves. He had got *that* title from the owner's penchant for reading best-selling novels. The flat was a junior library. He reckoned there were more than six hundred books in it – every room had its private bookcase; its personalised reading. The kitchen contained volumes on cookery; the lounge *Encyclopedia Britannica*, Shakespeare and poetical works with a scattering of Tolstoy, Marx, Hitler, Browning, Byron, Pope, Milton, Macaulay, Burns, Scott and Hemingway; one bedroom devoted entirely to Chandler, Moffatt, Runyon, Fleming; the master bedroom exclusively reserved for erotica and witchcraft.

His "fortune" was disastrously low now. His salary barely covered current expenses. He had coaxed Totter to suggest he deserved a higher stipend than starting pay and been agreeably shocked at receiving an extra four pounds a week. On reflection, he agreed with their new assessment of his worth. He had managed to pick up quite a lot of know-how. Totter could take sick or fade away any time and he would be able to carry on for a short period without help.

I wish the old bastard would die, he thought. *I could make a bomb from cooking those books!*

He shrugged off the thought. Totter could last for another decade at least. He was one of those dried-up old prunes who show their wrinkles but don't get older. Not mentally where it counted in accountancy, anyway! The infrequent slip-up was minor – certainly not a capital mistake like Joe hoped to come across.

With what he had salted away and what he got each week he could manage. Just! It meant dipping into ill-gotten gains but he did have an exclusive pad, a decent wardrobe, a swish address. He was all set up and rarin' to go...

*

Marissa Stone was celebrating her forty-fifth birthday alone. She knew the terrible frustrations of spinsterhood. At night, she lay in bed writhing in untold agony wishing a man – any man – would burst into her room and rape her. Her only sexual memory was the vicar near Oxford and even that had been discoloured by his wife's ghostly presence and the organ-loft trysting place which did not remotely resemble her pre-conceived idea of a nuptial bed. She had found the floor hard, unyielding. She had not been keen on baring her limbs to centuries old dirt nor to having her virginity taken in the midst of tolling bells and swelling organ music.

For all the enjoyment she felt there were a hundred displeasures to counteract the briefly concluded memories shared.

She had no comparison to judge her vicar by. She read startling modern novels and often attended the cinema where bare bosoms and panting cut-short scenes suggested more to sex than she and her vicar had ever experienced. She wished to know the full scope of emotional permissiveness yet lacked the gall to offer her flesh for just any young blood's lust.

In her search for fruition she had thrown herself body and soul into youth club activities. As a Sunday School teacher she felt she had accomplished enough to teach the youth of today where they had detoured from the "true path". Yet, she did not honestly understand where the same path took one.

She was a lonely woman wandering in the tracks of a celibate Son when all she wanted was *the* hot-blooded encounter with a Devil's Apprentice.

Marissa did not consider herself a hypocrite yet she was the acme of hypocritical disillusionment. She loved speaking of God's commandments but, in private, she absolved herself with nightmares voicing their disapproval of her chaste spinsterhood.

The club held nightly meetings in a former warehouse not far from Marylebone station. After two years operation, the trustees had managed to discourage certain Edgware Road types from venturing into their sanctum sanctorum. At first, brawls had been commonplace. More than one local alderman had demanded that the club be closed. But, with perseverance and a slow weeding-out process, they now enjoyed praise, support and approval.

In her capacity as a senior counsellor, Marissa Stone came into contact with every member. She formed friendships with those willing to take her advice yet not once had she dared to exploit those associations. Many a time she wished she could kick over the traces and have an affair with some of the athletic youths she dreamed of nightly. Always, though, decency forbade her the ultimate intimacies of man-woman relationships.

In a sense, she knew that some of the boys would have taken her to bed had it not been for her stern, uncompromising attitudes when more than a friend-in-need emotion began to raise its love-ly-ugly head. Truthfully, she was scared stiff of getting involved. Those lonely hours spent writhing in bed could not make her waking self condescend to having physical contacts with any of the young, virile, panting men. Much as she wanted them, there was a conscience-created barrier denying her fulfilments so extraordinarily sought after in the dark privacy of night.

Undoubtedly, she was an attractive woman. Age had not been unkind. She could still favourably compare with women ten years her junior. She had a slender appeal most men found exciting. Her breasts were still firm, her thighs solid and softly cool to the touch. Her touch. Mankind had yet to sample those delights in a comfortable bed. She had a pleasant face with warm, green eyes, a slightly sensuous mouth and silken honey-blonde hair. She was neither tall nor short and her clothes *always* were bought to please the opposite sex.

She had definite likes and dislikes and her political leanings sometimes shocked those liberals she was compelled to associate with as a youth club organiser. She did not believe the permissive society had to be encouraged. In fact, she did her utmost to foster old-time family pangs in the hearts of her converts.

Perhaps, she thought wearily, *that is why I am still a spinster; why those with whom I could glad-*

ly fornicate refuse to consider me an object of lustful dalliance...

*

Joe heard about the club in a roundabout way. One evening, as he relaxed in Terry's old Mayfair hangout, he happened to get drawn into a conversation dealing with Terry's sentence.

"You were his pal," a brash loud mouth said as he downed a pink gin. "Didn't you know he was a drug addict?"

Joe contemplated Vera's hidden navel and wondered if he should make the grade with her that night. She gave every indication of being available, willing, excited by the prospect of being his "mate". Their Tarzan-Jane mental clashings had aroused in him a desire to find out if she performed as well as she suggested she would. And yet...

"Terry wasn't addicted," Joe informed the group. "He never took drugs. A friend of his coaxed him into a one-time deal and it went sour."

"Come off it," loudmouth exploded. "People don't get coaxed into sordid things like narcotics."

"Have it your way," Joe sighed and signalled Vera for a refill.

"Do you take drugs?" the man asked next.

Joe swung on his stool. "Mister, leave me alone!"

The man inched backwards, eyes suddenly alert to his danger. Joe looked positively menacing. "Kids," he said covering his inability to match Joe's ferociousness. "Man, I wouldn't have a job trying to sort them out these days. I know of a club of drop-outs in Marylebone. It's supposed to make saints out of sinners but that's debatable."

Joe suddenly found himself interested. He had been searching for a youth club, or some fraternity catering for the modern society. He asked: "Where is this club?"

Loudmouth scoffed: "Don't tell me you're a do-gooder, too?"

"I'm not against progress," Joe answered in his best "Totter" retort.

Shrugging, the man dived into a pocket and withdrew a bunch of business cards. Sorting through them he singled out one. "That's it," he said nastily, reaching the card to Joe.

Committing the address to memory, Joe smilingly returned the card saying: "Thanks. I don't believe it's my scene…"

*

Marissa Stone studied the new arrival with a jaundiced gaze. She did not particularly like the mode of dress nor the supercilious air with which the newcomer considered her group. Getting to her feet, and making excuses she approached the youth and asked: "May I be of some assistance?"

Joe sensed her animosity towards him and smiled. He invariably enjoyed a clash of personalities. He didn't give a damn what she thought of him nor did he have to belong to this outfit. That's what made his attitude harden. "That's doubtful," he said. "I came expecting something more lively."

Marissa refused to let her feelings get the better of her. "What precisely did you expect, Mr 'Joe Hawkins.'"

Leaning on his umbrella he affected an upper-class frostiness – or what he hoped was the icy blast he sometimes got in the Mayfair bar. "I had an idea this would be some sort of sports club with nightly dances."

"Oh," Marissa said coldly. "We do have sporting activities and dancing but not every night. We try to act like responsible adults. All play and no work makes for weak characters."

"Tell that to the House of Lords," Joe sneered.

"Are you a communist?"

Joe laughed. "Do I look like a *Morning Star* reader?"

"People who answer questions with questions are usually afraid of their own convictions," Marissa said primly. "Mr. Hawkins, just what are you doing here?"

"I heard about this place and came to look it over," Joe replied with honesty.

"Are you seriously interested in joining?"

"That depends." He did not particularly care for the young people seated across the huge barn-like room. They gave him the creeps. Each one looked like a goodie-goodie – especially the girls.

"You think we might be too tame for you, is that it?"

He nodded. The woman appealed but he did not reckon her as a source of pleasure. Her type seldom indulged in extra-marital excursions. Anyway, she was old enough to be his mother. Belonging to an acceptable organisation had advantages but one had to weigh every aspect of a situation before being committed. There must be clubs where a preponderance of the members were full of fun and not a bunch of sour-faced mummies.

"I'd like you to try your strength against Brian over there," Marissa said softly. "I should inform you he boxed for this club against the best German competition last year."

Joe sneered. Who the hell did she think he was? Boxing didn't appeal any more than wrestling. If he got into a fight it would be on terms he dictated, not rules laid down by some moth-eaten old earl long since dead. Anyway, he wasn't a muscle boy. He had worked as a coal-heaver and developed hard, durable biceps. But being able to throw sacks of coal didn't necessarily make a man another version of Samson. He preferred to toss a bird around a bed and nurse his energies through a night filled with passion.

"I'm not a boxer," he said. "I can fight but not for fun."

"If you'd care to join us you might be agreeably surprised," Marissa said finally. Something about Joe attracted her. At first, she had felt nothing but detestation for his cocky perusal of their club. She didn't like his outlook but then, she very seldom found new members making a big hit with her. She was always willing to let a youth's personality grow on her. Surface values were not measurable guides to what lay inside. Many people presented a hardened exterior to shield themselves from the hurts a mercenary world invariably dished out.

"Alright, but don't expect me to like it," Joe said as he followed the slender woman across the room.

*

Basically Joe Hawkins had a "feeling" for violence. Regardless of what the do-gooders and the socialists and psychiatrists claimed, some people had an instinct bent on creating havoc and resorting to jungle savagery. Joe was one of these. Being part of a club which tried to foster a live-and-let-live fellowship did not weaken his desire to unleash brutal assaults on innocent folk. The club was a front to cover his deep, dark nature. A requirement for his suedehead cultism.

Unknown to Marissa Stone and the other adult workers, the Marylebone premises housed a growing collection of addicted youths. Joe found himself invited to join in extra-curricular activities which would have meant immediate castigation had Marissa heard the slightest whisper of what went on. It was as if Joe had been *guided* to the barn-like old warehouse. As if he had been fated to meet those others sharing his unsocial feelings.

Jeremy French came from a middle-class family shattered by scandal. Divorce and a succession of parental mistresses had sent him down the wrong road until, as a skinhead, he had been brought before a court and given a suspended sentence.

Larry Miller had always been on the "wrong side of the tracks" according to his story. His mother had been a gypsy, his father a lazy loafer unable to hold down any job for more than a month. When they moved into London from their native Birmingham, Larry had taken up with a gang and been its leader until the Uxbridge police had finally laid a trap and nicked them all with the sole exception of Larry. Since then, he had kept his nose clean but had not deviated from a life of minor crime.

Walter Spencer had never belonged to a gang and had never seen his home ruined by infidelity.

He had always been treated fairly and had been given the best possible education. Nevertheless, he had graduated into cultism from a sense of loyalty to his fellow teenagers and had grown to hate those things for which his family had stood. Decency, democracy, dedication to ideals sponsored by community committees held no appeal to his fertile brain which was totally devoted to the destruction of all that the elder generation considered "dear".

John Moore neither cared for life nor brotherliness. He hated because he did not get along with others. Although he formed an association with Joe, Walter, Jeremy and Larry he did not have any loyalty to them. No more than he felt it necessary to treat Marissa Stone as a benefactor. His entire attitude was one of "screw you, Jack – I'm okay." And he was okay, too. He had a highly paid position with an advertising agency, shared a flat with a sexy bird who loved him and got knocked about for her trouble, and had seven hundred pounds in the bank – a result of following form in *The Jockey*. John was no mug punter. He studied his nags, studied what the experts had to say and made an assessment from this. When he bet he could be sure of at least third place.

One thing Joe's crowd had in common was football mania. They did not support the same teams but they did stick together. Saturday was brutality day for each of them – be it at Upton Park, Stamford Bridge, Highbury or White Hart Lane.

A memory of getting "done" tormented Joe as he eased into Stamford Bridge behind Larry. They had agreed – no "Shed" today. They did not fit in "The Shed". Their clean-cut clothes, their aloofness, their lack of colours flying in the breeze would have invited automatic jibes – and worse. Chelsea's skinhead supporters had not lessened in their desire for trouble-making although great efforts to curb their vicious effectiveness was beginning to have results. The old days of outright slaughter had vanished as surely as bovver boots were a dying symbol of a passing phase.

Joe was happy to mingle with a more elite crowd than had been his normal Saturday afternoon wont. An umbrella did not stick out like a sore thumb here. Nor did those greying skies and weather forecast mean police suspicions as they entered the ground.

"There's a bunch of Chelsea fans," John exclaimed, pointing.

Walter grinned and gripped his umbrella as a General would his sword preparing to engage the enemy. "I see space behind them."

Larry and Jeremy were already pushing their way through the chanting crowd, climbing the steps to get on a level with the unsuspecting fans they had spotted. Yard by yard they advanced making room for John, Walter and Joe to squeeze through in their wake. Once, a woman screamed abuse as Larry trod on her foot but a growled oath soon stopped her cold. There was something threatening in those cold, detached faces to make her suffer in utter silence.

"This'll do," Jeremy announced.

Joe studied the position. When he had his gang his word had been law. No longer. The group he now found himself with refused to follow a leader. Each member was an individual, each permitted to voice his opinion without fear of contradiction by a "king". In the three weeks plus a few days they had been together they had agreed to remain loosely linked whilst keeping personal identity and personal choice. Their only concession to a union had been in a name for themselves. That had been Joe's suggestion although the name had come from Larry's mind.

"Marylebone Martyrs" sounded like an ancient rebellion in Joe's ears but the others agreed it was fitting. After all, as John had said:

"In ten years time there'll be dozens of gangs aping us. Maybe we won't make headlines but somebody will get to hear about us. They always do."

"The nearest exit is in the next aisle," Joe said softly.

Larry grunted and glanced over his shoulder.

Walter grinned, brought his umbrella up and removed the false tip which effectively hid its lethalness. Now he was a General with sword in hand!

John unscrewed the handle of his umbrella and withdrew a wicked little blade from the body. "Six inches of joy," John called his hardened steel toothpick.

"Watch where you jab that bloody thing," Jeremy snarled. "I don't want to be accused of murder."

"I can handle it," John replied indignantly.

The Chelsea supporters were beginning to howl as their team took the field. A scattering of Newcastle United fans sent up a valiant roar as the Geordies came into sight.

A police helmet moved back and forth across Joe's range of vision and he wished he had the guts to pig-stick the copper. The glare of publicity he had once adored did not appeal, however, and he concentrated his blind fury on the nearest Chelsea fans.

"Two... four... six... eight, who do we appreciate," a supporter hollered.

"Chelsea!"came the answer from a thousand throats.

Tension mounted within the packed stands. Newcastle won the toss and elected to play with the breeze behind them. The season was young and the teams suspect. According to last year's form, Chelsea should have an easy game but Newcastle were never a team to roll over and play dead for London clubs. They could fight hard and more than once took full honours back North.

Joe's umbrella snaked out and found a target. The man's anguished yell rose above his chanting comrades. By the time he turned, hands clasped to back of thigh, Joe was leaning on his umbrella with an innocent expression ignoring the other's hate-directed gaze.

"What bleedin' bastard stabbed me?" the man asked. Two of his fellow Chelsea mates were also facing Joe, anger darkening their heavy jowled features.

Joe tried to control a twitch in his left eye. "I beg your pardon?"

"You'll beg for bloody mercy you little..."

"Hey, Harry – look!"

The injured man tore his gaze from Joe. John stood with umbrella body clutched in one hand, wicked blade plainly seen in the other.

"It was 'im!" the third man yelled, surging forward.

Like greased lightning Larry sent a foot into the Chelsea fan's belly, his umbrella slashing upwards... cutting across the grunting throat in a perfectly executed motion.

Joe, not to be outdone, stabbed at the already injured individual, catching him in the forearm, drawing blood.

By now, the entire section was alerted to trouble. A sea of angry faces looked away from the pitch – Chelsea colours prominent on each neck or lapel. Jeremy, John, Walter and Larry were each engaged in unsporting contest – their umbrellas taking terrible toll on the opposition. Joe found himself pushed back as his companions fought a retreating action. In harmony, his weapon slashed and jabbed as the Chelseaites showed confusion in their sol-id-packed ranks. Joe didn't blame them. He would not have wanted to thrust himself onto a lethal blade or a rapier-pointed sword-stick.

"Exit fast," John howled.

Joe caught sight of the coppers. He took one final look, felt his umbrella bury itself in a soft buttock and pulled it free before hurrying after his fleeing Marylebone Martyrs...

CHAPTER TEN

BEFORE HE rebelled against society, Jeremy French had studied art. He had an ability which could have taken him to the top of the commercial profession but since dropping out, he had forsaken his sketching for a less ambitious position in the City. One evening, as the gang sat watching television in Joe's flat, Jeremy idly selected a pencil and paper and began to create a true likeness of Larry. In minutes, the gang forgot the TV and posed – one by one – for Jeremy's talented pencil.

"Can you letter, too?" Larry asked as excitement flushed his already highly-coloured face.

"Of course," came the egotistical reply.

"Then let's get together and make a code of ethics for the Marylebone Martyrs," Larry suggested.

"You know the kind of thing... We, the undersigned, believe."

"We, the undersigned, hate..." John corrected.

Walter sighed: "You advertising bods give me a fat pain."

"My boss would love to caress your pained area," John quipped. "He's as bent as hell."

"Did he sample yours?" Walter asked viciously.

John got to his feet, eyes narrowing.

"No fighting among ourselves," Joe said. "I don't want my pad ruined."

"Another remark like that and something will be ruined – *his sex life*!" John growled. "I don't..."

"Crissakes, shut up!" Joe screamed. "Let's concentrate on what we hate."

"Queers," John said pointedly.

Walter smiled, still provoking; "Advertising bods!"

"Skinheads," Larry voiced.

Joe glared at him. "That isn't... oh, yeah, I see. I hate social workers."

Jeremy sucked his pencil for a few moments and then said: "Marriage."

In rapid succession they had second thoughts, then third, fourth until, finally, John scowled and set his pencil down. "That is all. To cover this lot I'll need a bleedin' great sheet of board."

"Five boards," Larry reminded. "One each."

"How about a crest for the Marylebone Martyrs?" John asked with a watchful eye on Walter.

"You're the ad man," Joe said quickly. "Why don't you design something?"

"Agreed," Walter said sleepily. He was bored with the game. He felt in the mood for excitement followed by a good dose of sex. He'd taken a lot of booze on board that day and only fresh air, a dark alley confrontation and a bird in that order would bring him back to near normal. He did not give a damn about John or their efforts to avoid trouble between themselves. He would just have willingly slashed John's throat as some other unfortunate guy's. Drink made him particularly nasty and he realised this. Yet, it never stopped him from over-indulging his taste for liquor. "I'll see you blokes at the club tomorrow. I'm splitting."

"What about...?" Joe began and hesitated when Jeremy gestured him to be silent.

Once Walter departed, Jeremy laughed softly. "You could have caused a stinking' bovver, Joe. He's in a bloody-minded mood."

"Since when is he anything else?" John wanted to know.

Larry grinned. "Sore because he doesn't like advertising bods?"

"Watch it, mate."

"Shit! I'm not..." Larry shrugged. "Okay. Okay. Let's all behave like good little girls." He winked at Joe. "Any more Scotch, fellow Martyr?"

"Where's your money?"

"Do we have to fork out for drinks?"

"Bloody right. I'm not a charity. Two bob..."

"Ten New Pence," John corrected.

"Stuff those," Joe snapped.

"Right into my pocket," Jeremy joked. "I'll have one, too. A large one, Joe!"

"And that's three bob, mate."

"How long's it going to take you to finish those cards?" Larry asked Jeremy, as Joe attended to re-filling their glasses.

"A week – once John lets me have a design for our M.M. crest."

"M.M.," Larry mused. "That gives me an idea. A pair of lovely tits and the initials M.M..."

"Monroe's dead," Joe called as he went heavy on his drink.

"She's still something in my mind," Larry said thoughtfully.

"Can you do Old English lettering?" John asked their artist.

"Naturally!"

"Good. I'll give you a rough sketch tomorrow night." He took his drink, paid Joe and tossed it back. "I'm going home. I've got a hot woman waiting for me."

"When do we get to meet her?" Joe asked.

"Why do you want to?"

"Not to screw her, that's for sure," Joe replied fast. He didn't want John getting wild again.

"Why then?"

Joe thought he detected a trace of mischief-making in the repeated question. He shrugged and collected from the other two. With his back to John he said: "Only because we're all mates, John. If you ever wanted her to come along with us it'd be nice if she knew us by sight and name."

John scowled. He protected his bird jealously. He didn't trust any of these bastards. Not with anything and least of all with a woman. Under no circumstances would he ever invite Doris to join them. She was over-sexed and liable to get the bright idea of taking them all just for kicks.

"Get home to your woman, John," Larry said. "Leave us pathetic do-withouts to our booze." He grinned and waved a farewell which John accepted sullenly.

"Now we are three," Jeremy announced as the door closed.

"I'm bleedin' randy," Larry sighed.

"Who isn't?" Joe asked.

"We could visit Marissa and rape her," Jeremy suggested.

"Would she nark?"

Jeremy smiled at Joe. "What do you think? She's getting older and hotter between those lovely legs of hers. No, I don't think she'd grass. Fact, I honestly believe she'd appreciate what each of us could do for her." He appeared in deep contemplation, his pencil darting across another sheet of paper as his imagination went into high gear. When he finished the sketch he held it out and breathed fast. "God, if she really looked like that..."

Larry and Joe got to their feet and went behind Jeremy's chair. Joe felt sweat burst out on his forehead. If this was the nude Marissa Stone then he would definitely be interested in taking her to bed. Jeremy's talent was positively pornographic. The face belonged to Marissa. The body, too – from what they knew of it clothed. But what she was doing did not fit... or did it?

*

As Joe dressed, he glanced at Jeremy's masterpiece. The artboard was a good twenty-four inches long by twelve wide. At the top was a self-portrait of the artist flanked by photographically accurate sketches of Larry, John, Walter and Joe. Under this came the Marylebone Martyrs' crest – an elaborate creation faithfully reproduced from John's design showing a shield, quartered, with crossed umbrellas in the upper left field; five sets of nipples in the bottom right field; five hands reaching for a bottle of Scotch in the upper right field and a refuse bin with five pairs of bovver boots showing in the last, lower left field. Rampant above the shield were a man and woman – naked and definitely about to copulate. Below, curled like a banner, were the words: IN UNITY – NOTHING.

Then came their creed...

WE THE MARYLEBONE MARTYRS DO SOLEMN-LY SWEAR THAT WE HATE, AND ABOMINATE...

QUEERS

CHILDREN

LESBIANS

LANDLORDS

SOCIAL WORKERS

COMMUNISTS

SKINHEADS

CONSERVATIVES

HELL'S ANGELS

LABOURITES

PRIESTS

LIBERALS

RABBIS

ANARCHISTS

FUZZ

RUSSIA

BLACKS

AMERICA

VIRGINS
CHINA
RUGBY
EMPLOYERS
HIPPIES
BLOOD SPORTS
SERVANTS
PROTESTERS
CRICKET
WINE
YIPPIES
MAGISTRATES
MARRIAGE
TRADE UNIONISM

It's not right, Joe thought. *It's stupid wasting time on something so infantile. It could have said: "We hate everything" and be done with it. That's what we do hate – everything, and everybody except ourselves.*

Taking ten quid from his hiding place under the carpet, Joe wondered where he was going to get some extra loot. Totter had successfully blocked Joe's request for a salary increase. The profit from Terry's drug haul was fast evaporating. In a few weeks he would be back down to living on the pittance he earned which did not please nor even pay the rent. He had to find another source of income. An illicit one, too. He could not afford taxation on "capital gains"... He laughed softly. He should be so fortunate in finding a woman like John had – one paying her share and giving her all every night. That's what he wanted. Not a wife – they were burdens. A girl who liked what they did together and had a steady income. A girl he could boot out of the flat when she began to bore him.

Maybe... He sprinkled after-shave on his face and used the deodorant spray under his arms. He felt fresh after his bath – clean enough for the fastidious Marissa Stone!

Now there was a woman with money. Could he talk her into sharing a flat together?

His image in the mirror scowled. "You're a silly twit," he told the reflection mentally. "Marissa wouldn't dirty her belly for you!"

The hell with Marissa, and the Marylebone Martyrs. To hell with everything. He would visit the club, take a walk down Regent Street into Leicester Square and pick up a queer. They still hung out there, like they always had. If he went to the toilet – the public one in the Square – he was sure to be accosted. He'd play the game and nobble the bastard once they reached where the queer lived. No hotels for Joe Hawkins. That didn't let him see how much there was to steal. None of those fast masturbations in a locked toilet, either. He wanted money – not homosexual thrills.

God, what the hell kick do the bastards get out of men? he asked his conscience. *We like girls, don't we?*

His little man in the chest cavity did not answer.

Selecting his brown tie with the artistic squiggles on it, he finished dressing. The flat came complete with a cheval mirror and he studied his presentation with a critical eye. Not bad, he allowed generously. Terry will never know how much he has done for me!

His hair had grown and looked like pure suede which was hardly surprising since he'd been having a Mayfair barber treat it at an exorbitant cost. Even Vera had once remarked how caressable his hair looked. Not that it got her into his bed. He had refrained from pursuing cheap tarts since seeing a television programme dealing with V.D. The sight of a male organ ravaged by disease had scared the living daylights out of him. Now, he selected his bedmates with a fine toothcomb efficiency which left him frustrated more than relieved.

"Shit on girls," he exploded, and then, smiling into the cheval mirror, postured to get the full impact of his gear.

No umbrella tonight. No bowler, either. Just his suede hairstyle, brown shirt, brown tie, tweed jacket and cavalry trousers. He thought his orange socks did something for the outfit. Like the Oxfords did, too.

But the hidden glory was his underwear. God, if those sexy birds could see his mauve jockey shorts and specially dyed emerald green vest!

He felt naked without his umbrella and gloves, but Marissa had asked why he thought it necessary to carry his symbol of City gentlemanliness when he was supposed to be relaxing at the club.

I'm a gas, he thought as he went to the door. *I'm a real gas!* He had been listening to Mason Williams records and reading American private eye literature recently. He liked to affect Trans-Atlantic accents and dialogue. The East End words no longer jumped straight into mind when he was confronted by weird situations. He had matured and believed in his abilities to handle each and every problem in a sensible, unhurried way.

So many changes had worked their individual miracles on Joe since leaving prison, his old mates would have found it impossible to link the two personalities. Joe Hawkins, skinhead, had been an uncouth, uneducated lout drifting on a sickening tide of violence, drink and cheap tarts. Joe Hawkins, suedehead, was semi-educated and capable of affecting a partially-polished front whilst enjoying the charade of decent citizen even as he battered some innocent's skull to a pulp. Exterior-wise, the two did not match. The brash, cheaply clothed bovver boy certainly had no place in the City world of elegantly garbed, expensively clad *Mister* J. Hawkins.

Also, Joe Hawkins as a skinhead had been a member of a recognisable cult with strict limitations on what to think, what to do – and how to do it.

Joe Hawkins, the suedehead, did not belong to any classifiable fraternity, good or bad. His sort hated each and every amalgamation, belief and *modus operandi*. A genuine suedehead had neither creed nor association. He could form a loose friendship with those sharing his lonely existence and run riot in company for a brief space of time. He could not be a member of a gang, nor belong to a permanent process. The Marylebone Martyrs were, in fact, against what suedeheads held dearest – personal freedom to come, go and think as a hate-filled individual.

What had really altered Joe was his new-found penchant for books. He thirsted for knowledge and although profound novels and historical yarns went over his head, he did manage to broaden his mind – in a minor way – by devouring anything with a sex-violent theme coming from the States.

The mere fact he bothered to read was, in itself, a drastic change. A gigantic improvement.

Taking two large drinks he began to whistle. This was his night!

CHAPTER ELEVEN

MARISSA STONE lived in a suburban house with her own private entrance. She had resided there for three years and not once had she missed rent day by a second nor been accused of causing undue noise. She liked padding around in her stockinged feet immediately she got home. She kept her television or radio turned down to a whisper and although her bed creaked, she had taught herself to remain in one position all night.

When she allowed herself the luxury of playing the *1812* on her outdated record player she invariably got to thinking about her stereotyped existence. Having to care for those underneath her flat was not the way people were supposed to live. Always being considerate of others had never been returned. She could recall many parties down below to which she had not been invited and which had gone noisily into the small hours of a working morning.

Thoughtfulness should have been a two-way pleasure. It wasn't. And she knew she was considered a foolish *old* woman by her landlord. *If only I could alter my basic character*, she often told herself as she lay in her lonely bed and listened to a late film blaring its gunshots into the silence of her night.

As she opened the door of her upper flat, she wondered if Joe would take kindly to removing his shoes. Then, she smiled as her feet found each dark stair with Joe's progress behind her coming as a series of stumbles and muttered oaths in the lightless stairwell. She had intended asking the owner to have a light fixture in the upper hall – one she could switch on from the door. But her intentions usually melted into nothingness when it came time to make her request.

She reached the kitchen and switched on a light. She saw Joe's outstretched hand feeling for the side walls, his foot raised and poised in hesitation.

"I'm sorry about that, Joe," she said as he came steaming up the last five steps.

"It's dangerous," he told her. "Can't you get a tiny nightlight fixed down at the front door?"

She had not considered that possibility and made a mental note to have an electrician fit one. It shouldn't be difficult. And it could operate from the bell's battery. That way, she would not be breaking her tenancy agreement. Nor place herself in a position of eviction.

"I hope you like my home," she said, hands extended for his jacket. She wanted him to feel relaxed, completely at ease.

There was an atmosphere of female occupation which did not grab Joe too kindly. He preferred a totally masculine brutality in his home. Frills, lace and pastel colours were not exactly his cup of tea. He had to admit what he saw in a few glances put his parents' abode to shame. His mother had never known how to mingle colours nor did she have an artistic sense. In fact, Joe could truthfully state that his mother had been utterly devoid of taste all her life. Her idea of something smashing in the house was a cheap, garish table bought in Brighton one Saturday afternoon. Or plastic horses purchased in the local Woolworth.

"Coffee or tea, Joe?"

Her voice brought him back with a mental jerk. "Er... I'd like something stronger – if you have it?"

She refused to look shocked. "I have sherry somewhere."

Joe withheld comment. Sherry suited her fine but left him colder than yesterday's leftovers. "That'll do."

She switched on the light in her lounge and ushered him in. The colour television caught his eye immediately. He had not expected that extravagance. The room had a lived-in warmth to match her friendliness. Those green eyes, her silken honey-blonde hair and slender – yet desirable – figure went perfectly with the subtle shades and soft furnishings she had. He sank into a low, large, embracing sofa and sighed.

"I'm not much on entertaining at home," Marissa said. She crossed the room, kicking off her shoes automatically. "Do you like good music?"

"Not really. I'd take The Stones any day."

God, how awful!, she thought.

"Have you heard the latest...?" Joe started to ask.

"I seldom get to hear pop, Joe," she interrupted. Her hands caressed the sherry bottle. It had been seven... or eight?... months since she last had a drink. Maybe she should not let it go so long in future. All the kids seemed to imbibe with a frequency rate that amazed her.

"You're missing terrific stuff," Joe said unabashed.

"We all miss something in life."

"I try not to," he grinned, studying her figure with every intention of enjoying yet another of life's pleasures shortly.

"I envy you and yet I don't," she replied mysteriously. She carefully poured two glasses, wondering if she was exceeding the limit or being miserly.

"That's a rotten answer."

She handed Joe his glass and noted his frown. *Too little*, she thought. *Too late now to add more. Oh well – he'll surely accept a refill!*

"Joe may I say something honestly?"

He gestured with a generosity he did not feel.

"Those socks..." She shuddered visibly. "Must you wear them so loud?"

"Loud?"

"Orange!" The word came spitting from her mouth.

"I like 'em. I've got others brighter than these."

"Lord..."

He sipped the sherry. It was a cheap brand bought from the keg. He could tell his palate did not appreciate it... his only criterion on things other than beer and Scotch.

"Do you have a job or do you have a lot of money in the bank?"

She laughed. Trust Joe Hawkins to ask questions like that and expect an honest reply. She hedged. "Do you think I'm wealthy, Joe?"

"You've got a pile set aside," he allowed.

"I've got precisely two thousand pounds and I *do* work."

Joe rubbed mental hands. Two grand. That was worth chasing. "Are you an executive?"

"Not exactly, Joe. I'm in charge of a typing pool. I'm classified as a supervising typist."

"Does it pay much?" He took another sip of his sherry and placed the glass on a nearby table. He didn't want much more of that. It tasted sweetly sick to his tongue.

"Why are you interested?"

"No reason," he lied. "Just conversation."

"I get twenty-seven pounds a week after deductions."

He whistled aloud. "That's a lot."

"I've been with the firm many years, Joe."

"Is the boss a friend of yours?" he grinned slyly.

"That's unfair!"

"Sorry, I'm being jealous..." He let the remark sink in before adding: "I like you a lot, Marissa."

She tensed. *Marissa*, indeed. She got set to let go at him, but noticed his eyelids partially close as he stared pointedly at her bosom. *Oh, God – is this the one?* she asked in silent prayer.

"I'd like to kiss you, Marissa..."

She didn't speak. Instead, when he took her in his virile arms she let him drape her along the sofa so that he now assumed a masterful position above her. She watched his mouth come closer... touching... then... He took her sherry glass and placed it next to his on the table. He placed a hand deliberately on one breast and, as she moaned very softly, his open mouth closing over hers.

All her nightmares, her erotic dreams came surging to the conscious surface when his tongue invaded her mouth. She could not restrain her desire to experiment with this brazen, unmitigated young lecher. The doors she had kept so tightly shut burst open.

What a tit, Joe thought as he felt the firm breast swell inside his cupped palm.

He won't stop at feeling me, she thought when he pressed her back into the sofa and lowered his body on to hers.

His mouth tore from her greedy one. "Marissa... let me take your clothes off!"

"Joe... no! Don't... oh, darling Joe..."

She lay supine as he undressed her. Every revealment excited him tremendously. She had the silky flesh of a screen heroine, the maturity of a goddess. Touching her naked skin sent shivers coursing down his spine, arousing his manhood.

A kettle could not have boiled in the time it took Joe to whisper his lustful demands. Marissa writhed – eager as a teenage virgin for this marvellous youth's strident passion. His hands roamed her nudity everywhere; pleasing her, teaching her, bringing her womanhood to blossom-bursting beauty.

"Joe... the bed creaks," she moaned as he tried to pull her off the sofa.

"Let it!"

She pleaded. "Do it here, Joe... not in the bedroom."

"Beds are for what you're going to get," he panted.

"They'll hear us downstairs..."

"Let 'em... maybe he'll give his old woman what you're liking!"

CHAPTER TWELVE

"You've got to stop saying those terrible words, Joe," Marissa said as she cradled his head against her moistly warm breasts. "I can't stand them."

"What do you mean?" he muttered to a turgid teat.

"You know..." She refused to repeat his pleadings at the height of their mutual climax. It had almost ruined a delightful, exquisite moment for her when he began to four-letter her into wild spasms of glory.

"You mean f..."

"Joe!" She pulled back and held his face in her soft hands. "Please don't say it again. Please?"

"You're crazy."

"I'm not. I'm a lady, Joe."

Suddenly, he knew the difference between his East End tarts with their lavatory-wall language and the genteel taking of a superior woman like Marissa Stone. But she must have words for what they had done, for urging her mate to reach that exotic plateau when all but the pulsating togetherness seemed remote and immaterial.

"Joe... Joe... Joe!" Her fingers curled into his hair. "Let your hair grow long. I like doing this." She caressed his head, massaging the scalp.

His hand rested on her stomach. "I like this, too." He massaged her with newly aroused inclinations.

"You're a naughty boy," she giggled, spreading herself for his pleasure.

"The bed creaked like hell!"

She pushed his hand away and sat upright. In the semi-light of the lounge he could see her marvellous breasts and her slender body until it dipped invitingly under the sheet. "It did?" She sounded nervous, almost frightened stiff.

"You said it creaked – and it did!"

"Joe... stop! Don't touch me there..." She brought his hand above the sheet. "Oh, this is terrible..."

"Are you worried about the downstairs people again?"

"Yes!" She kicked free of the sheets, stood naked and unashamed in her confusion.

"If you want me to do it again...?"

She knelt on the bed, listening to the rusty creak. "I do, Joe – oh, God, I do!"

"Then find another pad!"

"It won't be easy getting a decent place for this rent."

"You could share my place..."

She blushed. "I could *not*!"

"Why?"

"It's out of the question. I just couldn't..."

"You'd like it every night, wouldn't you?"

She touched his cheek with fresh love tenderness. "Yes."

"Then move in with me."

"Joe, you're a darling but I can't. It wouldn't be right!"

"What the hell is right?" he asked savagely. "Listen, Marissa – we're good in bed together. I like the way you make it and you like getting me. Okay, so who cares if you're older and paying me rent..."

"Rent?"

"Sure – you didn't think I was wanting a wife, did you?"

She chuckled. "Joe, you're fantastic. All right, I'll think about your proposition."

He shoved the sheet back and got randy when he saw what she could offer. "Come here, Marissa..."

Willingly, she flung herself down on him, her hands as eager and as intimate as his. Pent up years surged to a forgetful surface and she wallowed in instantaneous thrills...

CHAPTER THIRTEEN

IT WAS surprising how little Marissa had to contribute. Her soul cried out for a kindred mate which it could never find in Joe. For the young man, Marissa was a frustrated old woman soiling her flesh in pursuit of youth's virility. They had nothing in common outside the bedroom athletics which both indulged in to demented extremes. Dishes did not get washed after the evening meal, so great was Marissa's desire to recapture those excruciating cadences Joe's love-making produced inside her long without body.

Once, after a lengthy session striving to bring the woman to full fruition, Joe remarked: "Can't you make it quicker?"

"Joe, darling, don't be greedy and don't ever be too selfish. Let me have the same amount of pleasure you're getting."

"Okay – but don't drag it, eh?"

Marissa sighed. "Can't you feel things building to a wonderful climax? Can't you hold back a few minutes until I'm with you?"

"I haven't got time for fancy stuff."

"Fancy stuff? Joe, you're so wrong. A woman enjoys being a plaything for a man's slowly emerging passion. You're so quick I get frightened. You can't just think it and have it happen, you know. There are so many beautiful sensations we can share if only you remember it's not just for me... it's for us both. Slow and easy is best. Modern slap-dash isn't letting either of us find the true wonder of love."

"I want to go to the pub, Marissa," Joe said as if that finished the discussion, the excitement his hand was sending through her loins.

"And am I supposed to stay here and wait until you come home drunk?"

"You can come with me."

"I don't like pubs."

"So stay at home!" He got from the bed.

"You're like all those Jamaicans I've ever met. A woman is a receptacle for their lust – nothing more."

"You're letting your bias show."

She got off the bed and stood stark naked before his admiring gaze. She knew he adored her body –

those sensual curves and her mature slenderness which could still perform sexual miracles his little trashy girlfriends could not begin to understand.

"Want it now?" he asked crudely.

"Not now – not tonight, Joe. You go to the pub and find a tart to satisfy your wham, bam techniques."

He put on his jockey shorts and his vest. She had already covered her essentials with a pair of cotton knickers and a bra. The need for getting-to-it talk had vanished. "You're a bitch," he said. "You profess to like everybody yet you single out Jamaicans for ridicule."

"I'm allowed to think the way I want, Joe."

He pulled his electric-green socks on. That she had not been able to stop. His socks were as important as the Crombie overcoat. Even in summer he felt it necessary to sport the coat. There were suedeheads who did not take kindly to bowlers and umbrellas, he knew. But none of the fraternity would ever be caught dead in "ordinary" socks. Regardless of all those statements to the contrary each suedehead had a large part of the skinhead left in his symbolic attitude towards recognition.

"Are you going to meet your friends, Joe?"

He glanced at her with mounting disgust. She was old enough to be his mother and every day saw her acting more and more like an instructing mother-hen. She had tried, unsuccessfully, to "beautify his thinking processes". She nagged when he went to football matches, when he got away from her demanding sexual possessiveness. It wasn't that he didn't enjoy screwing her – he did. But there were other woman equally qualified to relieve Joe Hawkins. Women who would not stop short because what he suggested was *morally* abhorrent. The vicar's ghost still haunted Marissa even if she denied it.

In the months they had shared his flat, Marissa had given him a new slant on life. She had taught him how to hate sections of the community without realising that she shared those aspects of the confirmed bigot. Joe had been unable to associate her work at the club with her very narrow views at first but the more she opened up the deeper insight he got. She was a frightened woman packed with vastly contradicting motivations. She liked to be seen as a neighbour, a "sister in need to the oppressed", a do-gooder without blemish, a social reformer. Yet, inside her fears manifested themselves in night's terror, she loathed coloured people, detested anything remotely connected with trades unionism, opposed blood sports, decried a widening of British involvement in Europe because "those foreigners will overrun us" and could not tolerate a different religious viewpoint.

All her pet hatreds brushed off on Joe. All her noble – but insincere – mouthings, left him untouched. The only really lasting impression Joe would ever have of her when they eventually parted would be the memory of her slender nudity writhing beneath him, of her almost insatiable desire for orgiastic completion.

"I asked if you were going to meet your friends, Joe?" she repeated with hands on firm hips, face drained of colour.

"What if I am?"

"You might be chasing after some little whore."

He laughed. "If I find one I'll do more than chase!"

"You couldn't... I won't allow this!"

"You won't allow it?" He moved across the untidy bedroom. "Listen, Marissa – you don't own me and you don't give me any bleedin' orders, either."

"You're mine," she said as tears suddenly trickled down her pale cheeks.

"I'm not, you know," he grinned deliberately provoking her. "Why don't you find an old man your age and screw him to death. That's what you want, Marissa – an old bastard willing to be henpecked."

"You're a rotten devil!" she screamed.

"Cool it, Marissa. I don't want *my* next door neighbours thinking what an old slut you are."

Her fists beat against his chest.

"I'll bet half of them don't believe you're my aunt."

She stepped back, stunned. "*Wh...at?*"

"I told everybody you were my aunt. You didn't imagine I'd have 'em believing I was getting off with some ancient biddy, did you?"

Her hands clawed wildly at her brassiere, yanked it off. Next she ripped her knickers and flung them into his face. Sharp fingernails raked down her magnificent breasts drawing trails of blood. "I'll have you arrested for rape," she moaned, swaying from side to side in a hysterical fashion. "I'll accuse you of perversions..."

An explosion erupted in Joe's head. Blind, red rage took a hold of his muscles and his clenched fist bounced off Marissa's jaw. Her eyes glazed but he didn't notice. Like a prize-fighter gone berserk he attacked, slamming her back against the wall, hitting, bruising, battering as she slowly sank to her knees. Even then his viciousness could not be checked. His toe smashed into her stomach, caught her full in the face. Only when her pathetic groans subsided into unconscious silence did he relent and step back to examine his handy work.

There was nothing beautiful about Marissa now. She was what he had said – an old woman bleeding and discoloured and ready for the refuse heap.

Joe felt terrific. The unleashing of jungle emotions did something wonderful for his savagery-starved system. It was like the days when the gang had taken brutal delight in mauling anyone stupid enough to stand in their way.

Washing the blood from his knuckles he finished dressing. Taking a final look at Marissa he frowned. "When those heal she can get the hell out of here," he said aloud...

*

Two hours later, Marissa Stone pulled herself to rubbery feet and staggered into the bathroom. Great racking sobs shook her when she saw the terrible condition of her face and flesh. A bath did not take away the aches nor lower the swellings. Naked, she reeled into their bedroom.

I must have been mad to let the bastard talk me into living with him, her mind screamed. *I've got to get out before he comes back...* Forcing her unco-operative body to act, she found her suitcases and threw clothes and belongings into them. Fortunately, her precious furniture had been stored in a warehouse. Joe had not been able to convince her she should bring everything to his flat. Maybe it had been a premonition that had saved her from having to stay in order to safeguard her life's belongings.

She did not care how she looked. She just wanted out. Fast. Dressing, she closed her cases, locked each securely and telephoned for a taxi. She would stay in a hotel until fit. She would inform the clubs she no longer cared to give of her time. She would report sick to work. She would hibernate until not one trace of Joe's handiwork remained. Then, and only then, would she re-enter a society for which she had nothing but contempt.

*

Joe slept like an innocent that night. Being alone did not bother him. When he first saw she had gone he had been crazy angry. But, slowly, her absence had assumed pleasant proportions. She had outgrown her welcome, her sexual hold over him.

"To blazes with her," he had muttered as his drifted off into that semi-sand heaviness when all things, all dreams can be seen with startling clarity.

CHAPTER FOURTEEN

PIERCE SAT unyieldingly stiff in his ornate chair, fingers steepled pontifically before his nose. "Mr. Totter informs me you've been returning from lunch smelling of drink, Hawkins."

"God almighty," Joe retorted indignantly. "One lousy beer to wash down a dry sandwich."

"That is not what Mr. Totter says."

"Then he's a liar!" Joe suddenly got a cold, crawling sensation racing down his spine. He knew, instantly, he had committed the great *faux pas*.

"That will be enough of that," Pierce said quickly. "I have never known Mr. Totter to castigate an employee without justification. Personally, I agree with his assessment of your condition. I have seen you looking the worse for drink, Hawkins. And heard your language, too... in front of the ladies!"

"A few little oaths," Joe pleaded.

Ignoring Joe's attempted reconciliation, Pierce unsteepled his fingers, lifted a paper and held it menacingly in front of his face. "If that were all, Hawkins!" he said behind the official looking document. "I requested our bankers investigate you and they have turned up rather a remarkable history..." His eyes darted to one side of the paper, fixed Joe with unflinching disgust. "You have been in prison, Hawkins."

"So what?" Joe felt no need now to hide his past. He was sick to death of Pierce's attitude. He was going to get the boot so why not enjoy himself.

"Your salary is being prepared. We shall not require your services any longer."

"I paid my debt," Joe growled. "But that wouldn't interest a snooty-nosed bastard like you or Totter. You think everybody has to be pure, eh? Like hell they are. You'd climb into bed with that sexy secretary of yours if she gave you the chance..."

"Leave this office at once, Hawkins," Pierce roared, the paper dropping from his hands. Coming to his feet, the stockbroker placed bunched knuckles on his desk and bent forward. "Young man, I could thrash the hide off you but I refuse to soil myself. However, a word of warning – if you are not outside these premises in five minutes, I shall forget my upbringing and give you what you most deserve."

"You and Santa Claus," Joe sneered.

Pierce straightened and moved round the desk. Something in his expression warned Joe he could do exactly as he said. Raising a hand in defence, Joe said: "Okay... okay... I'm going!"

"That's true," the man said grimly.

Watching Joe hurry from his office, Pierce breathed deeply. His age and health did not warrant such extravagant thoughts as he had nurtured then although he had meant every word. He was glad that Hawkins had not stood his ground. These young louts seldom cared for their elders. One blow could have sent him into hospital.

*

I've got two alternatives, Joe thought as he nursed his Skol lager in the remotest corner of the pub. Most of the regulars had dashed back to work leaving the unemployed, the problem drinkers and the expense-account layabouts to wait out the afternoon closing hour. *I can wait for Totter and follow him home and beat the bastard to a pulp for grassing on me. Or I can report to the Labour and draw dole. I'm entitled to do that. I got kicked out.*

A pair of young people took the table next to Joe's. The girl wore beads, a long mauve dress without shape or attraction, a band around her un-combed, straggling hair and a minimum amount of lipstick. Her bare feet certainly showed how much dirt London's streets held. Her companion was likewise barefooted, had the same colourless strag-gling hair banded in Indian style and there the re-semblance ended. He had a handsome face where-as hers was plain and pockmarked. He had a hairy chest peeping from under a loose, unbuttoned shirt and she was practically flat – with or without hair! He wore tight Levis and made no attempt to con-ceal an overly developed manhood.

Joe leant back and considered their way of life as against his. They could never get decent jobs in the City but then, maybe they thought he was up-tight being chained to the Establishment. One had to admit they were "loose people". Not hippies, cer-tainly. Listening to their muted conversation Joe could tell they were highly educated, completely extrovertish, distantly aware of his interest and un-caring for his opinion.

Bloody fools, Joe concluded. *Them and hip-pies, yippies, snobs, drop-outs, protesters, shop stewards, bus conductors, manual labourers, desk-jockeys, soldiers, shopkeepers, fuzz, skin-heads, Hell's Angels... the bleedin' lot! All stupid. All bastards.*

Finishing his drink, Joe pushed past the girl. She exuded some exotic scent which assailed his nostrils like a joss-stick would an opium hater. He was glad to gulp London's polluted air and smell the fumes belching from passing lorries.

It was late when he made his decision about the future. He would sign on the Labour, apply for a Social Security hand-out and do a bit of queer bashing on the side. Totter could go boil in his senile juices. Much as he wanted revenge he did not see any way of getting even without the fuzz clanging doors on him again. And that he was determined to avoid. He liked his freedom to pursue his solitary campaign against all humanity too much to give the law another opportunity to remove him from society's playground.

He'd make out okay. He'd wangle another job once he got a duplicate set of insurance cards. That was easier than explaining away why he had been dismissed from such a prominent City firm. He knew some influential men now. Those antique dealers in his Mayfair club must have use of a bright boy. He could cook books given half a chance. Or run errands for about £20 a week. Or learn the racket and set up for himself when he got a few thousand together.

A few thousand! That bleedin' Marissa had that amount. Why hadn't he treated her right until after she had parted with her loot? he asked his agitated mind.

Navigating a steady course from City to Mayfair and, when he found Vera alone in the club, back to his fashionable flat with its now totally masculine atmosphere he let several ideas run their winding road to that most deadly "detour" sign. No matter how tantalising the notion seemed at first light there was some dark dread which prevented him from fullest acceptance. He was not afraid of getting into trouble – just of finding himself in the dock before that same magistrate. He'd done his whack of nick. Once of that was ample.

Pouring a stiff drink he whooshed in soda and sipped it as he bathed. Refreshed, helping himself to another triple pleasure he changed into casuals – content to regard his symbolic Crombie and bright, plaid socks uniform aplenty. Counting his dismissal pay he frowned. With the dwindled cash he had put aside his finances had a decidedly bleak appeal. He had to get another nest-egg, somewhere.

Entering the warehouse clubrooms he looked in vain for Marissa. He had believed she would return by now. A new face smiled at him. *God, don't they ever get young birds to take these cushy jobs?* This one was older than Marissa, more motherly, more syrupy voiced. She advanced on Joe, hand out ready to draw him into her all-embracing, responsible arms.

"I'm Jenny Price," she said. "Are you a member?"

Joe smiled, ignoring the hand as he looked around for Larry. He was reminded of Vera when he first entered *her* sacrosanct barland. "Yeah, I've been here before. Seen Larry Miller tonight?"

"That one!"

Joe quizzed her with his eyes. She had a smug, almost omnipotent chastisementic expression going.

"I told him his sort are not welcome here!"

"Who the hell are you to say who can, or cannot, come?" Joe asked in sudden anger.

"I have responsibilities..."

"You're supposed to keep an eye on the equipment, the premises and help us if we ask for help. That's all – and don't deny it. I know. Marissa told me."

The woman blanched. "You're that beast Joe Hawkins!"

"You've heard about Marissa's shack up?"

"I certainly have. You may leave immediately."

"Shit on you!" Joe strode away. Down in the far corner of the huge room a couple of youths were heading a soccer ball. In the centre, several birds wearing stage tights tried to keep in step as an ex-dancer went through the weary motions of terpsichorean dilemma. A larger group of mixed sexes sat on the bare floor listening to an unkempt liberal spouting poetry and general blasphemy.

"Hawkins – come back!"

Jesus wept, Joe thought and continued to seek someone who might know where he could locate Larry. It was important. And he did not intend to have that old biddy scream at him for long. Her brand of authority was what his hatred was all about.

John Moore looked up, caught sight of Joe and left the "education circle". "What the hell is she yelling at?" John asked as he joined his mate.

"Not what – me! I'm not an honoured guest..."

"No bloody wonder. Where is Marissa?"

"Gone. Left. Where is Larry?"

"In the nick doing six months."

Joe wanted to weep. There went another of his big ideas! "And Jeremy?"

"In the coffee bar down the street."

Jenny Price swept up, hand gripping Joe's sleeve. Savagely he tore the Crombie material from her arresting fingers. "Leave me alone, cow!" he snarled.

The woman seemed on the edge of hysterics. John nodded and said: "Better go, Joe."

"Not until..."

"I'll call the police!"

Joe froze. She would too. He decided against further antagonism. "Okay, I'm going." Turning, he walked defiantly to the door. He was burning up inside. Only the threat of police action prevented him from asserting himself and giving the bitch what she deserved.

It had been a rotten day. Fired from his job, tossed out of his Marylebone clubhouse. Larry in the nick. He felt uneasy. Maybe he should go home and sleep off the bad luck dogging his heels.

Jeremy was chatting up a fifteen year old nymphet. He did not greet Joe with any enthusiasm. Now Joe was sure he would call it a day! A lousy day!

"Can you meet me tomorrow, Jeremy?"

"What time and where?"

"My flat after seven?"

"Have Scotch and American ginger."

Joe shrugged. He had both already. "Alone?"

Jeremy narrowed his eyes suspiciously.

"I've got something I wanted Larry in on but he's..."

"Out of circulation," Jeremy laughed.

"Yeah. Okay?"

"I'll be there. Say," as Joe started to leave the packed coffee bar, "where is that Marissa bird?"

"How the hell should I know?" Joe shouted in reply and pushed a long-haired girl aside. He did not hear her expletive nor see the coffee she had just bought trickle down her faded blue sweater. He had other things on his mind – like a drink and sleep.

CHAPTER FIFTEEN

"YOU'RE STARK, ruddy crazy," Jeremy remarked as he pushed his empty glass across the coffee table. "Make it larger." He deposited cash on the table with a show of disgust. If they were having a party or just shooting the breeze as the Yanks called it he did not object to paying his fair share for liquor. But when Joe had brought him to the flat and wanted to involve him in a highly off-beat, wild scheme it was etiquette to provide a guest with free drinks.

Joe scowled as he poured generous helpings of his best Scotch. He could not understand Jeremy's reluctance to jump at the opportunity to get some easy loot. Larry would not have hesitated. Of that he was certain. But Larry was not available and

Joe was in a hurry to build his nest-egg into an aviary-sized deposit.

"I still say it will work," Joe said, handing his companion the extra-large drink. "Bloody Pakistani bastards don't fight back 'cause they're scared of us. Hell, we used to bash 'em for kicks!"

"Used to is the operative phrase, Joe."

"What do you mean?"

Jeremy shrugged nonchalantly, sipping his drink before adding to Joe's consternation. He could not quite put a finger on the root cause of the retrograde step Joe seemed to be taking. He wondered if it had something to do with Marissa. Since she had shacked up with Joe, the youth had kicked over many traces.

Settling back in a comfortable sofa, Jeremy asked: "Mind if I discuss this fully?"

"No – what did you mean about 'used to'?"

"You brought up bashing Paki bastards. That went out when you turned away from being a skinhead. Hate them, get the boot in sometimes but don't revert to bovver-boys aggros and expect me, or us... to back you, Joe. We're beyond that. Making a 'hit' for hard cash sounds terrific but not when it's linked to the old methods."

"Bloody hell," Joe exploded, draining his glass and leaping across the room for a refill.

"What's happened to you recently, Joe?"

The question caught Joe unawares. He frowned, liquor spilling on to the cabinet top.

"Marissa wasn't all she was cracked up to be, was she?"

"She wasn't bad..."

"She made problems for you, Joe. She made you frustrated. And when she cleared out you fell off a cliff."

Joe mopped up the liquor pool. "What are you? A bleedin' head shrinker?"

Jeremy smiled tolerantly. Educationally, he left Joe miles behind. His ability to probe a problem and make a fairly accurate analysis came from an inherent knowledge of what made people tick. Joe had, in his opinion, created a sex-goddess and when that object of his worship failed to produce the vital pleasures in the abundance Joe had sought, something had snapped and thrown the youth into a tailspin. The result – backtracking and a desire to refashion a life-form long since consumed by time's forgetting fires. Joe as a skinhead now would be like a lamb amongst wolves.

"Are you going to help me?" Joe asked angrily.

"No, thanks. Count me out."

"Some mate you've proved to be."

"My advice to you is to drop the crazy idea, Joe. You'll get nicked. Things aren't what they once were. Pakistanis are acceptable members of every community..."

"You mean you like *them*?" Joe asked in amazement.

"Not me," the other replied hurriedly.

"Then let's do the job?"

"No – and that's final."

"I'll do it myself," Joe threatened.

"Fine. I'll send you a Christmas card to Pentonville." Jeremy climbed to his feet and finished his drink. "I'm shoving off, mate. Think over what I've said. You're muddled. Take a few days and get roarin' drunk."

"The hell with you and the Marylebone Martyrs... I'll get along on my tod."

"Bloody good luck, mate..." Jeremy snarled as he opened the door. Standing half in, half out he grinned evilly and added: "May all your troubles be fuzz!"

*

Sunday, and Joe's dilemma had multiplied instead of diminishing. The more he thought about Jeremy's visit to his flat the worse his mental confusion became. Word had circulated. The Martyrs no longer existed – not for him, anyway. He had been given the cold shoulder treatment by John and Walter. He had been "allowed" to overhear Walter say: "I hate skinhead punks and ex-skinheads trying to look like suedeheads." That had been the kiss of death.

Had Jeremy been right in tracing his failure to Marissa? Undoubtedly he had suffered at her hands. Those nights spent trying to make her react to his erotic suggestions had done more damage than he had thought possible. He could see it now – her mothering, her efforts to create in him something which was basically against his violent grain, her lack of compassion when he sought to get his hands on her money, her deep-rooted morality which refused to recognise things as they really were. She had been brazen about living with him. Her prejudices had been more volatile, more convincing than his shallow pretence to understand why everything should be classed as a suedehead hatred. He hated, true. He hated violently. Yet he did not hate with conviction as against Marissa's bigoted look at the world. Parts of her had gladly rubbed off on him. Other facets of her being had reacted with devastating results. He was caught between her good, her evil, and totally incapable of distinguishing a real Joe Hawkins path.

"I've got to do something or I'll go mad," he told his breakfast egg. He considered several Sunday possibles and brushed all but one aside. Hyde Park Corner... There would be blacks and Irish and commies galore there. He might be able to foment trouble. Maybe even a king-sized aggro...

He was thinking wrong again! He was *not* a skin-head. He belonged to the elite. All he required was a bit of *gentlemanly* bovver to rid his body of the ambition-eating cancer that daily grew larger.

*

"This is me – the real me," he mused as, flicking a speck of dirt from his velvet collar, he posed before a restaurant window outside Marble Arch Tube station. In his estimation he was a walking example of how the well-dressed socialite should appear in public. Crombie (with velvet collar), dark blue suit, brilliant yellow socks visible under his trousers, highly polished shoes, frill-fronted shirt, narrow floral tie and bowler perched jauntily on his head. The umbrella completed a picture of sartorial elegance.

Several tourists paused to chuckle as he passed them. A pair of hippy-types smiled behind his back. An elderly man blinked and muttered about fashion decline. A schoolgirl sighed and tried to catch his eye.

Joe was totally alone. He did not see the girl, nor the man, nor the hippies, nor the tourists. He walked with back ramrod straight, head high, umbrella swinging. His mind was already over there – in Hyde Park. Memories returned to torment him. Had he spat in the wind of fate? He felt a warm, satisfying glow permeate his being. Something was going to happen today. He sensed it...

The largest crowd was gathered around a rostrum flying a flag of a newly created African state. An ebony man wearing gaily-coloured robes occupied the rostrum, gesturing as he spoke in a loud clear voice.

"The Great White Queen sent her royal message-boys into Africa with orders to rape, and loot, and steal," he roared. "She sent us justice in place of gold taken from our mines. She made us slaves – for that's what her justice was. White men didn't get brought before colonial administrators for crimes committed against Africans. Only blacks were sent to penal settlements..."

"Liar!"

The speaker gazed at the back of the crowd with a huge grin displaying pearly white teeth. He had been waiting for somebody to object. He knew how to arouse a crowd and counted on his tirade getting a heckler going. Once a verbal battle began his audience would grow, and grow, and keep growing providing he could handle himself.

"Are you a student of history, friend?" the African asked.

"I'm English. We don't want your crowd here!"

"Oh, my," the speaker said, gesturing to his listening sympathisers. "I'm African, sir," he spoke directly to the hidden heckler. "Does that mean your people got out of my country and left me alone?"

Joe pushed through the thickening mass and placed himself defiantly before the rostrum. His umbrella waggled imperiously. "Your country was rotten before we took it," he shouted. "A bunch of savages who couldn't work or build towns..."

"Thank you, sir," the African interrupted. "Took it, you said. And that's what the British did. Took – by force, by underhanded deceit. We didn't ask you to come and occupy our lands. We didn't..."

"You hate our bloody guts yet you all flock here to get jobs," Joe roared.

"Why shouldn't we? You stole everything we ever had. We've a right to get it back."

"Not from me mate!" Joe screamed, his fury beginning to take command. "I don't want niggers in London."

"Niggers?" The African scowled, leaning over the rostrum. "Don't dare call me a nigger!"

Joe grinned sadistically and jumped forward. Like a spear his umbrella tip found a soft, fleshy target. The African's anguished bellow sounded like a cat-call to arms in Joe's brain. The umbrella slashed out catching an innocent bystander across the nose. Cracking bone increased Joe's desire to inflict pain. He lunged, aiming for the speaker's shoulder... Blood spurted from the man's throat as the vicious tip pierced his windpipe.

Joe suddenly blanched. He didn't like the way the man instantly sagged, nor the free-flowing blood, splattering robe and rostrum. A self-protective instinct sent him spinning into the stunned crowd. Eel-like, he wriggled from grasping hands trying to halt his progress. Cries for help rang in his ears. A police whistle drove him wildly into the heavy traffic circling the park.

I've got to get into the tube, he told himself as he dodged cars and buses in headlong escape. *The bastard deserved it...*

*

Monday's *Evening Standard* carried an Identikit picture of Joe. Underneath the likeness, an article condemned the violent society and those who would inhibit free speech. The writer – a distinguished legal mind – made no bones about his personal feelings. "Thugs like the one who deliberately attacked this coloured orator deserve to be put away for a very long time."

The front page, too, carried a report on the disturbance. Eyewitness accounts proved conclusively that the assailant had not been physically provoked. A police statement said that "The attacker is expected to be apprehended shortly". The spokesman hinted that "He is known to us".

He studied the Identikit picture as it accused from the floor. How the bloody hell could they know him? A picture taken during his skinhead era would not even remotely look like one of him now!

He had to admit there was a superficial resemblance. But then, it could have been any one of a thousand other suedeheads.

Okay, he told his tortured mind, *let's reason this out. Can they trace me?* He shuddered. Damn his rush to sign on the dole. They had a name and address there. If the fuzz were really looking for Joe Hawkins they'd have him!

Flinging his bowler across the flat, he dressed in casuals. The law was searching for a suedehead. They'd never stop him when he looked like an ordinary, decent citizen. He felt better immediately. Packing his Sanyo and some underwear into a small suitcase, he collected what was left of his cash and had a final drink. It was farewell to the flat. He could go north. Manchester had a going scene. In a few months the fuzz would forget him.

His hand was on the doorknob when he heard the solid feet approaching outside. Fear tore at his guts... *No! They can't have worked that fast...*

*

"...A menace to society which must be stamped out. Apparently you do not understand the meaning of leniency and so I shall safeguard the public for the maximum permissible by law. I sentence you, Joseph Hawkins, to four years…"

He was dead inside. The lengthy condemnation had stolen any hope he had entertained when entering the courtroom. Now, he knew. Four years! And that bloody inspector had mentioned another charge just before he was brought to face his nemesis. It seemed the queer had made a complaint. And the Sanyo had given him away!

"You're lucky that African didn't cop out," a stern policeman remarked as he took Joe back to the cells.

"Lucky?" Joe screamed. "I got four years!"

"Not a day too short," the officer grunted. "Take my advice son – have psychiatric treatment when you're inside. The world'll have changed drastically before you get out…"

Joe frowned. It had altered enough the last time he did bird. What would be the vogue when he stepped from those gates again? Would there be a new fad to capture his imagination? Or would he simply drift into crime *à la mode*? One thing he knew for certain – no headshrinker would examine him. He didn't intend to become a sissy. They could say whatever they wanted but Joe Hawkins would always remain Joe Hawkins. If he was wrong then he could only blame himself. He didn't want other people putting loony ideas into his mind. Next time he would capitalise on his experience...

"*Just like you did after eighteen months?*" a small voice asked...

THE END

SKINHEAD

(OPENING CHAPTERS)

CHAPTER ONE

OUTSIDE THE SHED, a freighter blasted the lunch-hour silence with her whistle. The churn-churn of props frothed the Thames as a Liberian registered vessel slipped from her berth, holds battened down on the vital exports bound for South Africa.

Inside the shed, surrounded by an untidy clutter of unloaded merchandise, the dockers relaxed – sandwiches eaten, tea brewed and being sipped, the flick-flip of cards the only sound they wanted to hear.

Jack Boyle grinned across the upturned crate at his mate Roy. "Whatcha doin', Roy?"

Roy Hawkins studied his cards for the fourth time. He wasn't much of a poker player. Solo was more his game. "Blowed if I know, Jack."

Ed Black leant across Roy's shoulder and snorted disgustedly. "Pack 'er in, Roy," he offered. "Let me take your seat an' I'll show you 'ow the game should be played!"

Roy glanced at Jack and got a nodded agreement in return. Slowly, he replaced his coins inside his dirty overalls, carefully stacked his hand on the discard pile and relinquished his seat. He didn't mind. He had only taken a hand because Ed had to see a union representative at the gates. "What happened about the meeting?" Roy asked as Ed slumped into his place.

Ed set twenty quid on the table with a flourish. He fancied himself as *the* poker player of all time. His claim to fame was his ten hour visit to Las Vegas when sailing the P. & O. line to Vancouver and Japan. He never let his mates forget how he managed to sit in on a game with Red Skelton and come out showing a profit of six hundred dollars. What he forgot to mention was his subsequent call at a Gardena, California club and the loss of that six hundred plus every British penny he had in his pocket.

"Jack's got 'em by the short and curlies," he said loudly. "They got until Monday to meet our demands..."

"And then?" Roy asked, stuffing tobacco into his old briar.

Jack gathered the cards and started to shuffle the pack. His attention was focused on Ed but it didn't stop him doing an expert job and dealing five cards to each member of the school.

"Then we go out," Ed announced.

Roy scowled. He didn't like strikes. He believed in Jack Dash; believed in a working man's right to withdraw his labour for better pay. He didn't believe in frivolous disruptions of work – and, in his opinion, this latest episode was decidedly petty. "I'm against it Ed," he said.

Black spread his cards tight against his chest. He was a canny man; a distrusting individual. He studied the cards pointedly then, having proved his superiority, glanced leeringly at Roy. "You'll do exactly as Jack says!"

Roy nodded. *Yes*, he thought, *I'll follow the bloody band. I dare not go against it.* He believed that Jack Dash was the man closest to God; believed fervently in the right of the docker – and every working man – to take measures to combat the capitalistic employer. He was completely disenchanted with this Labour government – but he wouldn't abstain nor vote Tory. He would vote Labour as he always had; as his dad and his granddad had. It didn't matter what he said between elections – that the long period of Tory rule had been the best in living memory – providing that when the day came, he could make his "X" against the local Labour party candidate. In his constituency, Plaistow, the ineffectual hands on the helm of England counted for less than a man's worth to an employer. 1926 and the "cloth-cap" image had to be preserved. Forgotten were the affluent days of Tory rule. Forgotten were the massive debts piled on a staggering nation by yet another Labour administration. It didn't count that Britain was being dictated to by the International Monetary Fund.

"Are we playin' cards or discussin' the political situation?" Jack Boyle asked.

Ed Black glanced at his fellow-docker.

Roy smiled, puffing contentedly on his briar.

Solly Goldbluff smacked a fist into his palm and demanded, "Fuck the politicians and Jack Dash. I've got a hand – when are we goin' to play cards?"

Ed glared at Solly now, relinquished his platform to the determination showing on that Jewish face. He had never understood Solly; just as he had failed to appreciate Roy's hostility to the Labour movement as specified by extreme adherents like Dash. He knew that Roy would follow along in the main-stream of opinion; knew that Labour had an unswerving vote from Hawkins; knew too that the disenchantment Roy felt was common to the majority of trade unionists. Yet, he was assured by "cell" leaders, Roy and his mates would vote as usual when the crunch came.

Studying his cards, Ed shouted, "I'll open..."

Roy watched the game with lessened interest. He saw his mate win the pot; saw four other hefty hands go to Jack. Then, suddenly, it was time to return to work.

"It's a bleedin' shame," Jack Boyle said as they stepped outside the shed, "that Ed has it in for you, mate."

Hawkins shrugged and puffed on his pipe. "Oh, he isn't so bad."

"Like hell! He's a rotten bastard…" Jack's antagonism boiled over as Ed stepped from the shed with four of his special cronies trailing behind like bodyguards, ready to prevent physical harm to their adored leader. "Why don't you let Joe do him?"

Roy ignored Jack's suggestion. It was enough that he claimed fathership to the lad. He didn't have to be reminded what a rotten little bastard his son was nor to inflict him on one such as Ed Black. Basically, Roy was decent; law-abiding within the limits set by dockland. He did not consider pilfering a crime; it was a docker's perks to purloin Scotch and foodstuffs and the occasional costly items from "broken" packing cases. In the old days, Christmas would have been a barren table if it hadn't been for the goods stolen from the docks. Mostly, the employers and the police turned a blind-eye to the petty stealing. Only the capitalistic insurance concerns made a hue and cry about the extent of dockland thievery. Like so many of his mates, Roy didn't stop to consider that £10 a month taken from somebody else's pocket could multiply into a fantastic sum when set against the total number of dockers in the nation.

"'Owabout it, Roy?" Jack insisted.

"Forget Joe," Roy growled. "I have..." He tapped the tobacco from his pipe and prepared to mount the gangway of a Norwegian freighter.

Boyle frowned. He couldn't understand Roy's attitude toward his own son. In his opinion, Joe Hawkins was only doing what all of them should do – have a go at authority. Jack was a rebel out and out. Only his hatred for Ed Black saved him from being classified as a militant – plus, of course, his friendship for Roy. He needed somebody like Hawkins to temper his viciousness; his addiction to causing trouble.

An hour later, Jack found himself forced to work with Ed. In a far corner of the hold, Roy slaved with a dedication Jack found sickening.

"Christ, doesn't 'e know when to stop?"

Ed Black welcomed the opportunity to take a break. He wasn't a man who enjoyed hard labour nor did he consider it necessary to kill oneself for the employing body. His creed was simple – "higher pay for less work." Productivity agreements were, to him, a means to an end. They sounded fine on an engineering contract but, in reality, they meant absolute zero in action. His brother in the *Mirror* had kept him informed of *their* productivity agreements and it was a family laugh when they discussed the way that union had buffaloed the government's prices and incomes policy.

"'E's a blackleg, Jack. I don't trust 'im."

Boyle moved away, wishing to hell he hadn't opened the door for another Black tirade. Roy and he may not always agree, see eye-to-eye, but they were mates. Which was more than could be said for Ed Black. Ed was nobody's mate. "I wouldn't annoy Roy unless you want to meet up with his son, Joe."

Ed jabbed a finger into Jack's chest. "That little bastard isn't interested in the likes o' me. 'E ain't even worried about 'is old man."

"It isn't wot Roy said," Jack threw back, hopefully. "I wouldn't annoy Joe Hawkins. Not ever!" He shook his head thoughtfully.

Ed Black was thoughtful too. He was big, strong, had taken care of himself in some weird corners of the globe. As the union representative, he could count on certain heavies to protect him during a strike. His cronies would always rally round his particular flag, too. Yet – the mention of Joe Hawkins sent a shiver of fear down his spine. He couldn't understand this modern generation. Violence was a natural part of life as a docker saw it but the style of brutality these kids employed frightened him silly. Fists and the occasional kick happened; clubs with nails sticking through, and boots specifically meant for inflicting serious injury, were something else again. It wasn't just Joe Hawkins that worried him. One yellow-spined kid would never worry the likes of him. But Joe had a mob and even he was forced to admit that one man was no match for a bunch of savage little bastards ready to tear an individual apart just for fun.

"I'll talk to Roy," Ed said softly, moving away from Boyle.

Jack grinned. Slumping against grain sacks, he waited for Ed to return. When the union specified it took two men to lift what an old-time docker would have considered an easy weight, Jack believed in obeying rules. Two men it would be; and every lost minute meant a fatter pay-packet anyway!

Joe Hawkins hated his parents with all the violence in his young body. Especially, he loathed his father's attitude to life. What, he asked himself as he washed meticulously, had his dad gained from being a soft touch? The house they lived in was far removed from a palace. It was small, cramped, in an awful street. The neighbours were old, foulmouthed and unintelligent. Not that Joe felt that he possessed a good measure of intelligence. He admitted, but only to himself, that his education had suffered badly. But he was foxy clever. He had a native intelligence that would carry him to heights his father had not inspired to reach. Plaistow and its dirt were not for Joe. One day, he would move away and never return. His sights were set on a plush flat somewhere near the West End. But that required money, and social position. And, as yet, he had neither, although his day was coming. Of that he was positive...

"Joe... you upstairs?"

He turned from his wardrobe mirror and scowled at the partially open door. His mother sounded in a vile temper – as usual!

"Yeah."

"Come down 'ere."

His hand automatically reached inside his shirt for the comforting feel of the tool stuck in his trousers' waistband. He was proud of it. He had taken a week to make the weapon – thick rubber tubing filled with lead-shot and sand, and plugged securely until it was pliable without losing the necessary sting when used. Dropping his shirt over the cosh he slowly descended the narrow stairs.

"I arsked you to fetch me bread this mornin'," his mother snarled. She waved a loaf before his face, "'and over the money... this is stale!"

Joe grinned. "It was all they had."

"The money!" Mrs. Hawkins said again, hand outstretched. Joe didn't frighten her. She was one of those heavy women with massive forearms and a determination to match her girth. She had been born in Plaistow and fought for everything she had.

All her life, Thelma Hawkins had known poverty and hardship. Unlike her husband Roy, Thelma did not have cause to trust her neighbours nor believe in anything except herself. Even her son was an object of suspicion where it came to money.

"I ain't got it," Joe sulked.

Thelma's heavy hand swung, catching the lad across his cheek. "Joe," and she breathed heavily, "I'm not arskin' a second time."

The boy's hand dipped into his pocket and handed over a coin. Thelma sighed, fingered the coin as a priest would a statue of the infant Jesus. "Next time I arsk you…"

"I won't bleedin' go!"

Returning to his room, Joe contemplated his face in the mirror. Her hand-marks showed red. "The old cow" he muttered, fondling his cosh, wishing to hell he could get enough courage to use it on her. Pleasant dreams flooded his mind – and, he saw his hand streaking down, the cosh a blur as it slashed across her cheek, the sound of cracking a satisfactory end to a fleeting wish.

He fingered his face momentarily, then swung from the mirror with an exclamation of frustration.

Opening the wardrobe, he selected his gear from its shadowy recesses…

Union shirt – collarless and identical to thousands of others worn by his kind throughout the country; army trousers and braces; and boots! The boots were the most important item. Without his boots, he was part of the common-herd – like his dad, a working man devoid of identity. Joe was proud of *his* boots. Most of his mates wore new boots bought for a high price in a High Street shop. But not Joe's. His were genuine army-disposal boots; thick-soled, studded, heavy to wear and heavy to feel if slammed against a rib.

It was Saturday and West Ham were playing Chelsea at Stamford Bridge. He wished the match had been at Upton Park. A lot of his mates had stopped travelling across London to Chelsea's ground. Funny, he thought, how the balance of "power" had shifted from East to West in a few years. He remembered when the Krays had been king-pins of violence in London and the East End had ruled the roost. Not now! Every section of the sprawling city had its claim to fame. South of the Thames the niggers rode cock-a-hoop in Brixton; the Irish held Shepherd's Bush with an iron fist; and the Jews predominated around Hampstead and Golders Green. The Cockney had lost control of his London. Even Soho had gone down the drain of provincial invasion. The pimps and touts there weren't old-established Londoner types. They came from Scouseland, Malta, Cyprus and Jamaica. Even the porno shops were having their difficulties with the parasitic influx of outside talent.

Like most of his generation, Joe *knew* about these things. At one time, East Enders enjoyed a visit to Soho and mingling with the "heavy boys" from Poplar and Plaistow and Barking. No longer. The word had circulated – stay away from Soho. Look for your heroes in Ilford, Forest Gate and Whitechapel. The old cockney thug was slowly being confined – to Bow, Mile End, Bethnal Green and their fringe areas. London was wide open now. To anyone with a gun, a cosh, an army of thugs.

Joe was brash enough to venture forth into enemy territory. He had seven mates – all tooled for trouble; all asking the same question: "Any aggro today?"

Slipping a light-weight cotton jacket over his gear, Joe studied himself in the mirror. The cosh didn't show under the jacket. He fingered his West Ham scarf, then threw it back into his wardrobe. *That* would be asking for police inspection... and the last thing he wanted was having his cosh found before he had an opportunity to use it.

He wasn't a bad-looking youth. At sixteen, he gave the impression of being at least nineteen. He was tall for his age – five-eleven. He had filled out and, at a fleeting glance, many a young girl's heart would flutter when he appeared on the scene. But his eyes could have deterred those females wary of sadistic companions. There was something in his gaze that spoke of brutality and nonconformity expressed in terms of physical rejection and explosive reaction.

At last, he was ready. Taking a final glance at his appearance, he nodded to his image, grinning approval. Then, with heavy boots making a resounding noise on the worn stair-carpet, he went to the front door, yelled: "I'm goin'," And left.

Outside, on the street, he paused.

God, how he hated this street! Next door, he could see that bitch Grace peeping from behind her curtains. What a bloody bitch she was! No matter how he acted, nor what he thought, he hated her for the way she had treated her husband. In a way, though, he was afraid of Grace. In his opinion, she was a black witch – and he didn't want to associate with her!

He hurried down the street, conscious of eyes following him. It was always the same. No matter how early he left the house, eyes always followed him. Sometimes he wondered if they ever slept in his dirty street.

He was whistling when he strolled down to the Barking Road. The cosh felt comfortable against his flesh. His boots felt solid, secure on his feet. In a few minutes he would meet his mates and, soon, they would be ready for aggro...

CHAPTER TWO

Fresh air in the pub was more valuable than gold dust. Smoke from countless pipes and smouldering cigarettes filled both bars, effectively helping to dull the clinging smell of cheap disinfectant. Nobody had ever asked the guvnor to list his establishment as a must on a tourist itinerary. It was unlikely anyone ever would.

If air was precious, a sentence spoken without four-letter emphasis was enough to bring sudden silence, raised eyebrows and get the speaker an award for bravery in the face of obscenity. Even the two barmaids spoke in anatomical descriptiveness and some of their suggestions were physical impossibilities except for a mechanical engineer.

His mates had the Saturday corner table and Joe shoved through the crowd, catching sight of Henry Downy at the bar. "Pint, mate," he yelled, getting a nod from the pimpled youth. Frankly, he couldn't stand the sight of Henry. The guy's pimples wanted to make him throw-up. Not just that, though – he had serious doubts about Henry's usefulness to the mob. He had always kept a close eye on Henry's activities and never ever gave advance information of an aggro when Henry was listening.

"You tooled?" Billy Endine asked nervously as he took his chair.

"Of course," Joe replied with an indignant sneer. "Think I'd go to fuckin' Chelsea without this?" His hand fondled the cosh under his shirt.

Billy shrugged and watched Henry struggle through the crowd with their beer. None of the boys tried to help the pimpled youth. It wasn't part of being mates to offer a helping hand. Not in their mob, anyway. "'Enery ain't got 'is!"

Joe fixed Henry with a malicious eye. He watched how the beer slopped on the table as the other nervously set it before him. "Wot's this about you not 'aving a tool?"

Henry glanced over his shoulder then spoke in a whisper. "My old man found it. Jeeze, didn't 'e raise hell!"

"You're a bleedin' liar, mate," Joe said deliberately. "Go get a tool or forget the game." His hand closed possessively round the glass, his mocking smile destroying Henry's unspoken reply in advance. As the pimple-face youth walked dejectedly away, Joe laughed. "Serves the bastard right! Drink up lads... 'is beer is good!"

From behind the bar, Mary Sommers watched the group. She couldn't take her gaze off Billy and, she felt sure, he was returning her interest each time he glanced across the pub. She was nearly old enough to be his mother but it didn't stop her having physical yearnings for him. It hadn't made her say no two weeks previously when Billy accosted her after closing. Nor had she tried to get away when he seemed to tire of feeling her. In fact, she could admit to herself that it was her prompting that had seen their confrontation develop into a frantic mating behind the soaring Point flats.

She knew she was asking for trouble getting involved with one of them yet her knees shook when she thought about how wonderful it had been pressed against his hard young body. Looking at Joe and the others she even wished Billy would waylay her tonight and share her with his mates. The escapade with Billy had opened floodgates inside her; made her realise how tame the past ten years had been with a man who really never gave sex a thought. She could remember when she was eighteen. Her proud boast then had been "I've been screwed by every man in the district". Since her marriage, she'd had about six bits on the side – hardly enough for a healthy, passionate woman with her shape.

Bending to pour a pint, she became aware of eyes peering down her wide-fronted blouse. She looked up, and caught the old lecher leaning forward to see more of her breasts. He turned away, smiling secretly. He'd had his eyeful and that was his fair share. At seventy-three a man could look but not touch.

Mary shrugged, her breasts jiggling firmly. The motion did not go un-noted. Those closest to the bar grinned; those at tables tried to catch her act but she refused to co-operate, her attention still rivetted on Billy and his mates.

"You don't want little bastards like them, Mary-girl!"

She swung on the man. "Mind your own fuckin' business," she snapped.

The man frowned. "Christ, lads – she's really after Joe!"

Let them get it wrong, Mary thought, flouncing down the bar. They'll be trying to catch me with Roy's son and I'll be rubbing against Billy. *God*, she sighed. *I wish I was!*

"That old cow!" Billy snorted disgustedly. "I jumped her an' she raped *me*."

Joe twisted round, studying Mary with a lascivious eye. He had to admit she looked pretty good for a tart. Turning to Billy he grinned. "Was it good?"

"I've had worse."

"Arrange to meet her and we'll all be there…"

Billy frowned. "If she hollers, Joe…"

"Bloody hell, she's only a wet-knickered bitch! She won't holler. Go ahead – talk to her."

Billy got to his feet looking dubious. It was one thing trying to get a bit in the dark for yourself, he thought, but letting Joe and his other mates share – well, that was asking for big trouble. Since hanging had been abolished some magistrates were getting bleeding horrible with the amount of porridge they handed out. Especially when it involved tear-aways and girls! Bloody M.P.s, he thought. They got elected to do what their constituents wanted done and the bastards thought they were little tin-gods better than the voters! If he had his way every politician would be slung into prison and given a taste of what they deserved.

"Hey, Mary…" He leant against the bar between two huge coloured men. The stink of the blacks made him sick. He hated spades – wished they'd wash more often or get the hell back where they came from. This was *his* London – not somewhere for London Transport's African troops to live. He enjoyed the occasional aggro in Brixton. Smashing a few wog heads open always gave him greater satisfaction than bashing those bleeding Chelsea supporters.

Mary slopped beer into a glass and pushed it at her customer. She felt her knees go rubbery. Collecting the cash, she rang it up, then hurried along the bar to face Billy. Her eyes sparkled, her breasts heaved.

"Same again for the lads," Billy muttered, unable to tear his gaze from those beauties. It wasn't his round yet he couldn't come right out with the proposition. Joe's insistence on making Mary made him think about the other night and he suddenly realised how good it had been. Why should he share her with his mates?

"Billy wants to see you again, Mary..."

Billy glowered at Joe standing beside him now. Mary didn't flinch. She stared at Joe, asked softly, "Will you be there too?"

Joe nodded.

"When, Billy?"

The boy was lost. He couldn't understand a woman like her. He'd had his share of the little bits hanging around the fringes of their mob – the local girls trying to snare one of the better-known heroes. He'd even gone to bed with a Soho brass when they'd pulled a job off. But that had been a big disappointment. He'd felt sick, feeling around a professional tart.

"Tonight... when you finish here?" Joe asked.

Mary felt her throat constrict. She glanced up and down the bar. "Wait for me behind the Point?"

"We'll be there – won't we, Billy?"

Billy wanted to object. Knowing Joe, the woman would be subjected to extremes of intercourse before he – or any of the others – got their share. Yet, nobody denied Joe Hawkins his glory. "Yeah, Joe, that's fine."

Mary lowered her voice. "Forget this round – it's on me."

Joe laughed, returning to his seat. Mary would fiddle it. They were getting free beer on the guvnor for promising to give her what all concerned would thoroughly enjoy – especially Mary. The round was on her and everything else pleasurable would be on her, too.

The coloured man beside Billy laughed throatily, slapped Billy's shoulder. "Man, you'se got it made," he grinned.

Billy brushed the hand away and glared at the man. "Don't ever touch me, spade!" He backed away, ready to grab his tool.

Quickly, the two coloured men stiffened and moved to close in on their opponent. Then, suddenly – as the pub grew deathly silent – they glanced around and relaxed with foolish grins on their ebony faces. Even they had heard about Joe Hawkins, and his mob.

"Trouble, Billy?" Joe asked eagerly, watching the coloured men with what amounted to hungry appreciation. Like most East End skinheads – and, for that matter, population – Joe detested the influx of immigrants into what had always been a pure Cockney stronghold. It wasn't so much the colour of the skins that annoyed him. Any intruder would have been subject to the same treatment – be the man South African, Canadian, American. The East End was proud of its London-heritage; afraid to lose its ancient right to control what was, essentially, a Saxon bastion. 'Anglo-' had never been acceptable here. Loyalty to an established, accredited Cockney crown was taken for granted. In time of war, the East Ender had only to enter a recruiting office to be accepted as a fit example of a British fighting man. Nobody dare question that. Nor the right an East Ender had to voice his opinion regardless of Race Relations Board and governmental sympathies. Spades or wogs didn't count. They were impositions on the face of a London that should always be white, Cockney, true-British... not so-called British because they claimed a passport and insisted on rights their independent nations did not grant to the inhabitants of the British Isles.

"No trouble, man," the first immigrant said.

"None," his fellow black murmured.

Joe grinned evilly. He wasn't satisfied to let it go at that. This was Saturday – a day for splitting skulls. What better warm-up than these two coons...

"Apologize..." he suggested antagonistically, moving forward with his mob stepping in tight like a gang of Nazi S.S. men about to interrogate a prisoner.

Billy grinned. He felt tall, more than equal to a couple of hefty niggers now he had the backing of Joe and the lads. "Tell me how sorry you fuckin' well are," he snarled.

The first negro blanched. He lived in Plaistow and knew how difficult it could be to oppose this gang of young thugs. He had heard of other immigrants whose homes had been terrorized. He had been warned by the pastor not to invite racial discontent with the 'ignorant' Londoner. Mentally, he rejected these white savages – and all Englishmen – as inferiors striving to prove their right to subjugate black peoples. He didn't stop to think about the poverty and superstition that made his homeland a place to avoid, or leave, nor the debt each of his people owed to the British administrators, the British tax-payer, the British sense of fair-play. He forgot these things because he wanted a job, a decent home – even if, after occupation, he turned it into a slum-dwelling – and a right to stand on his own feet without having a witch-doctor, a tribal chieftain, or an arrogant headman telling him what to do, when to do it, how to do it. He remembered his rights in England – the right to protest and call the British bastards and exploiters.

"I'se sorry, *boss*," he snarled.

Joe laughed. "Boss? Sambo – get stuffed!" He turned away in disgust. The Chelsea mob would offer more resistance.

Billy puffed out his skinny chest and pushed past the coloured men.

Conversation started again in the pub and Mary's eyes glittered frantically as she kept watching Joe, Billy and the mob. These were her type of men, she thought. She loathed serving blacks. She detested their lecherous looks, their arrogant attempts to strip her across the bar and the almost "don't dare refuse me" propositions they made. But the guvnor had warned her not to invite trouble by refusing to serve them.